Killing Casanova

Traci McDonald

This edition published by
Crimson Romance
an imprint of F+W Media, Inc.
10151 Carver Road, Suite 200
Blue Ash, Ohio 45242

www.crimsonromance.com

Dedication

For Erik, who shows me every day what a man who truly loves you looks like.

Acknowledgments

My deepest thanks to my sister Kamarie for being the best cheerleader a girl ever had.

To Alyssa Shrout, the best writer I know, and the best friend I could ask for. I'd be lost without you.

To Virginia, for teaching me how to be not just a writer, but a good one.

To my editor, Jennifer Lawler, and the Ladies in Red at Crimson Romance, thanks for all the great ideas and for all your patience with the blind lady. You guys are great.

Special thanks to the Utah State Offices for The Blind and Visually Impaired, the Utah Chapter of The National Federation of The Blind, and Freedom Scientific for JAWS, their screen reading program.

Chapter One

"Jake." The honey-sweet voice drifted over the raucous sounds of the bar. Jake gulped down the last of his melted-ice-cube drink and turned back to check his reflection in the mirror behind the bar. The DJ was throwing back the rest of his drink too and preparing to start the next dance set. Jake ran his fingers through his hair, tousling the dark curls off his brow and watching the approach of a group of women behind him. Someone sultry had called his name, and he grinned crookedly, hoping it was one of these girls.

Four pairs of sparkling eyes probed his reflection, and he winked teasingly, drawing their long, tawny legs in cut-off jeans toward him. They were like a pride of golden-tanned lionesses spreading out for their attack, and Jake smiled more broadly as they skirted the crowd to close in on him.

Spinning on his stool, he cast his gaze back into the crowd as if looking for something or someone else, knowing that his lack of attention would just speed their descent on him. From the corner of his eye, Jake caught the flounce of blond curls and green eyes as a sultry form slid next to him at the bar. Possessively clutching his knee, she draped her slim, delicate hand onto his thigh and then moved his knees apart with her hips.

"Jake?" Her whisper prickled against his ear. "You're not going to dance with those little . . ."

Natalie Harper's voice paused ever so slightly, as she glanced pointedly at the women closing in around him. A wicked smile curled her lips as she looked back at Jake's reddening face, waiting for his mind to fill in the unspoken insult, before she turned his stool until he faced her crimson lips.

Natalie was beautiful, nearly six feet tall with eyes the color of the Irish hills. She put her other perfectly manicured hand on his other leg and pressed her curvaceous body against him, speaking in low, sultry tones.

"You belong to me tonight, Jake."

Twisting the stool back until he once again faced the dance floor, he forced Natalie to stumble along with him. Jake leaned his forearms back against the brass bar behind him.

"I'm drinking, Nat," Jake hissed, pulling as far back from her as possible. "Not dancing."

Natalie stood straight now, causing the pendant of her long silver chain to disappear into her cleavage. The white tank top she wore clung to her slightly sweaty body and Jake bit back a scowl as he watched more than one pair of eyes follow the heart-shaped bobble as it vanished, along with a single drop of Natalie's sweat, beneath her plunging neck line. She scowled openly and crossed her arms under her breasts, tapping one of her sandals impatiently.

"That drink's gone, Jake. I'll disappear a lot faster than those ice cubes if you don't dance with me."

She leaned across Jake's steely gaze, revealing the nestling pendant, before plucking the ice cube from the top of his glass. Holding out her tongue to catch the dripping droplets and then sucking it into her mouth, Natalie straightened once more, smiling demurely. Hearing the sharp intake of more than one man's breath, Jake fought the temptation to roll his eyes. He took the half-empty glass from the bar beside him and pulled an ice cube out as well, throwing it into his mouth and grinning at her.

"You better get going then," he teased, "I've only got two more to go."

Tonight had been Natalie-free—until now—thanks to his friend Lilly Pinion. Lil had been keeping a close watch on the blond bombshell by conveniently keeping herself in Jake's arms whenever Natalie was prowling, but now Lilly was off somewhere stalking her own herd of small-town cowboys, and Jake was on his own. Three and a half weeks ago Natalie's body and her lips had tormented Jake to distraction until he had spent some real time with her. Without the flashing lights of the bar and the too loud music, he had discovered the best part of kissing her, which was the only part with any appeal for him: it kept her from babbling relentlessly about . . . everything . . . nothing.

With another cocky grin, Jake picked up his glass and shouldered his way into the pressing crowd, not worried about Natalie being well-cared for in his absence. Jake found the swinging doors to the parking lot and pushed out into the night air. The roiling heat of the desert would soon be upon them, and the eighty degree nights would not last until June.

He had promised Heidi one last camping trip out to Navajo Canyon, and his mustang, Deseo, was chomping for one more run through the high meadows of the Sierra Nevadas. It would have to be soon, before the summer slaughter and the haying had to be done. Jake smiled wanly at the flirtatious glances of a few late-arriving teenage girls, but he did not move from his inclined position against the log wall of Mcgoo's. He had come home to help with the summer work at the cattle ranch, but the restlessness inside his heart could not be quelled tonight, and he was certain the glass in his hand was not chain enough to keep him here much longer.

Turning back to the pulsating music and lights of the interior, Jake saw the blur of Natalie's long hair again, and he slipped through the doors, along one wall and into a chair at the back corner table.

Deeper shadows hid his piercing blue eyes, and he leaned the chair back on its hind legs to sink further into oblivion. He had held, danced, and talked to at least three-quarters of the girls in the bar tonight hoping the usual distraction of their desperate attention would calm his heart. Gary Burke, his agent, had left him three text messages and four voicemails in the past three hours; his phone vibrated in his pocket to remind him that he had ignored them. He didn't want to think about that tonight, and he certainly didn't want to focus on life decisions with so many lovely distractions pulsating around him, but here he sat alone in a dark corner avoiding both the decisions and the distractions in favor of . . . ?

Jake watched Carter Langdon carry four longneck bottles of beer through the back door of the bar, apparently out onto the delivery dock of Mcgoo's. He would have to keep watch on Carter tonight; that guy was dangerous with too much alcohol—and he had passed "too much" an hour ago.

Steve Burwell appeared at the table in front of Jake and set down a chilled glass of lemonade on a paper coaster.

"Put that chair back on the floor," he growled, glaring at Jake.

Jake set the chair back on all four legs and grinned broadly at the grumpy old bartender.

"Sorry, Steve," he said. Steve straightened and folded his beefy arms across his massive chest as he scrutinized Jake's apologetic smile.

"What are you doing back here, Jake?" the bartender asked with narrowed eyes. "Your fan club can't find you back here in the dark."

Jake drank another ice cube from his empty glass and smiled more broadly now. "That's the point, Steve-o," he said with a chuckle, "I need a break from the fans."

Steve grimaced and glanced back toward the floor, stiffening slightly as the song ended and the dancers returned to line up at the bar.

"Don't make a fuss back here," he warned, pointing a finger at Jake and stepping aside to allow an auburn-haired girl to sit at the table. Steve glanced nervously at her, and then turned his back on Jake.

Jake smiled again, watching the bartender's usually stony manner soften into putty as he spoke softly to the girl and then moved a lemonade into the palm of her outstretched hand. She smiled warmly and tenderly patted his arm, bringing on a flush of color Jake had not known was possible in the graying features of the long-time bartender. He choked back a laugh before Steve could hear him and then looked at the girl.

She was pretty, but not spectacular, especially in comparison to the immaculate beauties surging throughout the room. Her long, wavy auburn hair was sun-streaked blond in places. Not highlighted in a sink somewhere, but truly streaked with flecks that were the result of long days in the sun. Her features were soft and pretty, but she wore no makeup and her eyes seemed too pale for her tanned features. They were blue, or maybe gray? It was hard to tell in the dim lights.

As she sipped slowly on her drink, light from the dance floor turned her eyes a pale sky blue. Jake shuddered a little at those eyes. They rested on nothing and seemed to see everything all at once. He turned away from them before she could catch him watching. Sliding his chair back away from her table and further into the corner, Jake looked everywhere except at her. The quiet hum of her voice caught him by surprise.

"You don't have to hide," she said with a soft laugh. "I don't bite."

Jake blushed openly at her quiet reproach. He should have known she would have been watching him, and he would not have been able to make even the slightest movement away from her without her noticing. He was surprised he had stayed hidden in the back corner this long without one of his entourage finding him.

"It wasn't you," he assured her with a cocky grin. "I'm not hiding, just looking for a quiet corner to take a break in."

"I'm Cassie," she said, holding out a hand in his direction but not moving toward him.

"Jake," he answered, leaning forward and shaking her fingers briskly.

He slumped back into his chair quickly, and she withdrew her offering with a slight wrinkle of her forehead.

"It's nice to meet you, Jake," she said sharply, turning her back on him. "Enjoy your break."

Jake grimaced guiltily; he was being rude and he knew it, but he was not interested in more swooning females tonight, at least not until Natalie had suspended her hunt. It went against everything his mother had ever taught him about respect and honor to hide behind her and insult her casual friendliness at the same time, just because he was in a bad mood.

Standing swiftly and moving his chair so he was hidden from view of the dance floor but close enough so she could hear him, Jake sat back down and spoke softly over her shoulder, "I didn't mean to be rude," he said, letting his voice drip with sincerity. "I am hiding, but not from you."

She gave a quick shake of her long hair, and Jake thought he heard a small laugh from behind her glass of lemonade. Sipping the drink slowly and then carefully setting down the glass, she turned ever so slightly in her chair. She focused her eyes on a dark-haired young man sitting in a chair just beyond the circle of dance floor lights and spoke as if she was speaking to that distant figure.

"This is a good place to hide," she said bemusedly. "That's why Steve put me back at this table. He says in a place like this you stay in the shadows, because the lights bring the snakes out at night."

A crooked smile teased her lips now, and Jake chuckled darkly. "Steve didn't know I was curled up back here tonight, or he probably would have found you another table."

"So what snake are you hiding from?" she asked, keeping her face turned slightly away from him. Jake lifted an eyebrow. If anyone were to glance over to their corner, it would look like she was talking to someone at another table, and he would remain cloaked in the shadows.

"She's not a snake," Jake said dryly. "She's more like Medusa."

"Medusa? Is she trying to seduce you or just turn you to stone?"

Jake scowled, looking around the room for Natalie. "Not sure. I guess it depends on if she's trying to hook up again, or punish me for not wanting to."

He looked back at the girl's face, expecting a smile and more of her easy banter. Instead her face was serious and now she turned her pale blue eyes boring directly into his.

"Well," she said tartly, "I guess that makes you the snake then."

A flash of white-hot fury danced in the depths of her eyes and she turned her back on him once more.

Jake sat stunned, shocked. Had he said something besides the words he had heard come out of his mouth? Had he accidently told her he'd been making out with Natalie because she was hot, and it was easy? Somehow he felt as if he had confessed the last month and a half of empty, casual relationships, and now she had hung the string of broken girls around his neck like an albatross. Jake opened his mouth to give her a defensive retort but found it already hanging open. What did he need to defend to her? Who was this girl?

"I'm sorry," Jake drawled, sarcasm heavy on his lips. "Mother Teresa? Is that what you said your name was?" Not even a flounce of her hair met his retort, and Jake frowned dejectedly. "Look, Cassie?" he said standing and shoving his chair back from the table. "This is a bar. This is why people come to bars. If you're too morally superior to the rest of us, then I guess this is the last time either of us will have to put up with each other."

Jake picked up his glass and drained the last of his melting ice before slamming it on the table again. His dark, stormy gaze caught the flash of Natalie's green eyes from across the room and he groaned under his breath as she started to move around the room toward him.

"I don't think you're in hiding anymore. It sounds like your tantrum has brought you out of the vipers' den."

Jake cursed quietly, then slipped back into the shadows along the wall and out the doors once more.

Chapter Two

"Jake or Dylan?" Cassie Taylor muttered, shaking her head emphatically as he slipped out of the club behind her. He was right, this was a bar, a bar in a small, lonely part of the Mojave Desert. None of these people were here for stimulating conversation.

He didn't know her, and still he had tried to do his best Prince Charming impression. She laughed at her own foolishness. Guys who were doing their best impression of anything had real demons to disguise and she was the last girl in the room any fairy tale writer would have chosen to cast in the role of princess. With a heavy sigh of disappointed reality, Cassie turned back to her lemonade and let the music drift to her ears.

"Cassie!" Jana Pembrooke said with a huff as she sank into the chair Jake had vacated. "What did you say to Casanova that made him so mad?"

"What makes you think I said anything at all?" Cassie asked innocently.

"Because he left, and he's the reason I dragged you out here tonight. He just started ignoring Natalie Harper, which means I, mere mortal that I am, actually have a shot with him. Now he won't be back, and I never even got a chance to introduce myself to him."

Cassie turned to face Jana now, feeling chagrined for ruining her friend's night. "Are you sure we're talking about the same guy? That guy's name was Jake, and he doesn't really seem like someone who has much going for him. A little grumpy, a little testy, and a whole lot arrogant. I'm sure there is a lot of decent guys here, Jana. What's so great about him?"

"Jake Caswell is the hottest thing in all of Lindley." Jana sighed. "Not that it says much, but he's hot enough to be an actor and a model in LA. He's only here between jobs, helping his dad with the cattle until he has another project out there."

Jana's voice was straining in pitch, and Cassie heard the edge of frustration plucking at the girl's patience. "He's gorgeous. That's why the girls around here call him Casanova. He smiles and asks you to dance and there's no resisting him."

Cassie rolled her eyes and grinned at Jana. "I managed it," she teased smartly. "Besides, I'm sure he'll be back next weekend. He's got to keep up that reputation with the girls."

"The next two weekends, we're taking groups to the campground and the river. It will be at least three weeks before I get back here, and I don't think Jake needs to come here to keep his social life full. Tonight could have been my last chance before he goes back to LA."

Cassie shook her head again. "I'm sorry, Jana. I just couldn't listen to him blame this girl for wanting to go out with him because he had hooked up with her and then changed his mind. He probably made out with her until he got tired of her, or got a better offer and then decided she was crazy or smitten because she misunderstood his intentions for her."

"He told you that?" Jana asked, clasping Cassie's arm in her hand.

"No," she sighed. "I guess I kind of assumed that was what he meant when he said some girl was either trying to seduce him or punish him."

Jana laughed again and pulled Cassie to her feet. "It sounds like you have known a few Casanovas of your own."

Leading Cassie through the crowded bar to the swinging doors and into the parking lot, Jana wrapped one arm around Cassie's shoulders and headed them toward the sound of departing vehicles.

"Yeah, a few," Cassie muttered as Jana pulled the keys from her pocket.

"I don't know Jake very well," Jana said, unlocking Cassie's door. "But from what I've heard, he'll either make you have feelings you can't fight, or he's the one your mama always warned you about."

Cassie frowned again and waited for Jana to start the old truck. As Jana backed out of Mcgoo's parking lot, Cassie sighed again. "Either way, Jana," she said sadly, "if I were you, I'd run for my life."

Chapter Three

"Yake!" The screech of Heidi's voice topped the highest volume setting on his car stereo. Jake kept his eyes on his phone, fingers flashing in quick movements between the Facebook and Twitter apps as he filled his dance card. His mother had frowned when she had called it that, but she had also promised to keep Heidi off his back long enough for him to take care of it.

"Yake, can you hear me? Are you okay?"

Heidi was talking to him, even though her tongue struggled to say his name.

"I'm fine, Heidi."

With a firm smile, he watched carefully to make sure the panic in her eyes faded from the other side of the car window. Heidi was mildly autistic; both her questions and the answers she expected to hear were literal. She did not ask Jake if he was all right because she was irritated that he was ignoring her; she asked because she was genuinely worried that he didn't answer because something was wrong.

Heidi scowled disapprovingly, and then put her hands on her thin hips. She was seventeen and had the dark eyes and long, lean figure that his mother still had even though she was in her late forties. Even with that frustrated look on her face, Heidi was beautiful, and the reality of it frightened him every time he looked into her deep blue eyes. His mother had always told him that God protected special spirits like Heidi's from the destructive powers of the devil; that's why Heidi's mind was so sweet and clear. She was an angel with human wings.

Jake frowned even as he thought of his mother's starry-eyed description. Human angels should not have been given the type of body that attracted the scum he knew were waiting out there for sweet innocent girls like his sister. The dark swirling lights of the dance club he had just been making arrangements to visit flashed across his mind.

Jake cast that thought aside as he turned off his stereo and rolled down the window separating him from Heidi, reassuring her with the removal of the barrier. The spark of light dancing in her eyes poked at him again as he silently justified his night games. He was just going to let a few lucky women feel . . . special . . . for a little while; he would never take advantage of someone like Heidi.

He pulled the keys from the ignition and then motioned for Heidi to step back from the car door as he opened it and unfolded his long legs from the bucket seat. Stepping from the car and slamming the door, Jake stood his six-foot two-inch figure up against the silver Mitsubishi.

"What's wrong, sweetie?" Jake drawled in the husky cowboy voice Heidi always softened for.

Last year Jake had starred in a magazine spread for Mustang men's cologne, and the local TV stations picked up the web commercial the company made at the same time. Heidi had seen him on television and thought he'd left home to go run wild mustangs across Wyoming, instead of in Las Vegas shooting the commercial. Now whenever he pulled the cowboy from his repertoire, Heidi would always forgive him. Most of the women around their small rural area recognized him from that commercial, too, and it had the same effect on them. Well, not exactly the same. Heidi was terrified that he would go back to Wyoming because he liked horses more than her. That was her complaint every time Jake even hinted about running the mustangs. The others just couldn't resist his brilliant blue eyes or his rugged features. The rough bad boy look and tall, muscular frame always did the trick. He could almost see knees buckle and hearts melt if he just gave them one of his signature smiles.

Drawing his fingers through his dark tangle of hair, he waited for Heidi to stop quivering her lower lip.

"I'll keep my promise, Heidi, but it's not time to go yet." Jake soothed, flicking his palm toward the sky. "It's still light out, and they can't do Cinco de Mayo fireworks while the sun is up."

Jake straightened from the car and put his arm around Heidi, pulling her back toward the house.

"I know, Yake," she said. "But Miriam said I could help with the barbecue if you would take me before eight, and it's seven already."

Jake did not falter or let her escape as he moved swiftly toward the kitchen door to deposit her back in the ranch house.

"Why are they having dinner so late?" Jake asked, trying to distract her.

Heidi was not giving in, and she spun out from under his arm to stand glowering at him, arms crossed and feet planted in the gravel.

"Miriam hired a new counselor at the ranch, and she needed all day today to settle her. We all need to help put the party together, that's why I have to be there as soon as possible, Yake. You know how much work it is without Yason."

Jake grimaced guiltily with her final statement, casting an abashed glare into the graveled road. Jason Sorenson had owned The Rocking J ranch since Jake could remember. Last year, Jason had been killed when his horse had broken its leg and fallen into the rushing flood waters of the San Madera River. Miriam Sorenson was saddled with a mortgage and an autistic boy of nine. She could not run the training and breeding facility by herself, and she had needed an alternative, quickly. Using grant money, Miriam had turned the former horse ranch into an equestrian therapeutic service center.

Heidi had become the beneficiary of not only the soothing constancy of the specially trained horses, but the friendship of the Sorensen family.

Now Jake crossed his arms and met his sister's pleading look.

"Come on, Heidi, I'd have to take you all the way out there, and then come back to help with the heifers. I've got plans tonight, too."

Heidi made an unhappy sound at the back of her throat but said nothing, letting the tears of disappointment brim her dark blue eyes. Jake closed his and sighed, dropping his hands helplessly at his sides.

"Okay, Heidi," he mumbled as she wiped her lashes clear. "Go get in the car."

*

Jake glanced at his phone again as he dropped Heidi by the bleached white rails that ran the length of The Rocking J's long drive. Cody Sorensen was counting the spiny rails along the western fence line to calm himself in the chaos, and Heidi went to walk the length of the fence with him.

The early May night was lit by a fraction of moonlight, along with the Chinese lanterns Miriam had pulled out of storage from the New Year's party. Parties were now a monthly occurrence at The Rocking J from the time Cody was diagnosed, making it a part of his regular routine and exposing him to the situations that encouraged coping. The consistency helped Cody adjust to the constant influx of owners and trainers that Jason staffed and supported on the ranch.

Miriam's new calling with horses made staff adjustments and clientele a never-ending surge of confusion for Cody as well, and the parties actually brought him normalcy. A new staff member would have thrown Cody's day way off, and Jake smiled ruefully watching his baby sister walk patiently beside the young boy. The clear evening and the twinkling lights marked an unfettered path for the two companions as they made their way toward the driveway.

Jake turned the Mitsubishi around without going up the drive to the cluster of women and ranch hands crowding the wide front porch. Heidi and Cody were in their sights, and Jake had chores to finish before he could shower and go into town to Mcgoo's one last time before the spring cattle drive tomorrow.

In a ranch community at the northern tip of the Mojave desert, Jake was lucky to have the old steakhouse-turned-bar-and-nightclub to fill his evenings. Lindley was just enough of a town to keep the locals bored and the old timers kicking. When Jake had left after high school, it was the last bump in the road he ever wanted to see again, but four years later his father's final words had come back to haunt him: "Sometimes the last place in the world is where you'll find yourself. Especially if you didn't know you were lost."

Jake flicked a glance in the rearview mirror as he checked one last time on Cody and Heidi before turning westward toward Caswell Farms. *I'm not lost,* he mentally argued, *just waylaid between lives.* The life he had planned when Melinda, his high school sweetheart, was still here. And the life he called his own.

Prickling fingers of starlight broke the black of night as he found the constellation Cassiopeia in the early summer sky. It was no more a constant than she had been, but somehow he still searched for both of them. Tonight, he wouldn't worry about any of that. It would be a week before he'd see anyone except the hostlers and cowhands. He would make tonight worthwhile.

*

"Jake?" a gravelly, mildly frantic woman's voice crackled over his cell phone. Jake pulled his hat from his head and mopped his sweating brow with the back of one arm. The sounds of lowing cattle and clamoring hooves drowned out the woman's voice, and Jake moved away from the trucks to hear better.

"Jake, it's Miriam Sorensen. Your mom said I might be able to get hold of you at the pasture. Can you hear me?"

Jake glanced around the rocky peaks surrounding the spring grazing land and wondered at his cell phone reception. He and the other hands had been unloading the last of the cattle for grazing. The dry, hot summers would starve and parch the herds on the desert floor. The few heifers that had calved on the ranch were being brought to the lush, green valley at the base of the mountain range. His father wanted a herd of forty or so brought down for the summer slaughter as well, and they had to transport those back to the ranch.

"I can barely hear you, Miriam," Jake said with one finger in his other ear. "Is everything okay? Is Heidi okay?"

Jake glanced around quickly as Carter, Troy, and Derek finished securing the gates on the trucks behind him. His father had hired the hands to bring in the spring stragglers, but he had insisted Jake go along to supervise. Jake turned his back on the young men as they began pulling beers from the back of the ice chest they had lost no time retrieving from the creek. He suspected the drinking was why Robert had sent him along. Troy was one of The Rocking J's men and Carter took orders from no one, not even Robert, but Jake knew the land and the work well enough to keep the guys working even if loyalty was not among their priorities.

The high meadows were plush and green, the aspens and firs filtering sunlight and the bright rays warming their days without freezing their nights. This was the only place Jake felt steady. The world was always tilting beneath his ever-changing life, and here, firmly standing on the bedrock of the mountain, the sky settled into a vast expanse of endless peace. The drinking and shouting of the hands and Miriam's voice on the phone sent the earth tumbling again, and Jake braced his back against the trunk of a broken tree to listen to her.

"Heidi's fine, Jake," she explained quickly, "everything is fine, except that . . ." Miriam's voice broke suddenly and he heard the edge of panic creep from her broken heart. Every time the ranch overwhelmed her, cruel pain darkened her brown eyes, and he heard her longing for Jason without her saying his name.

"It's fine, Miriam," Jake soothed in a quiet husky voice.

"Whatever it is, it'll be fine."

Miriam took a breath, firm tones returning to the call. "Actually, I'm hoping you can help me with that. There is a group of blind kids coming in for a trail ride and campout this weekend. I was only expecting a half dozen or so, but I found out today that there are nearly twenty teen-agers coming." The edge was crawling back into her voice now, and Jake blew a heavy breath into the phone. "The staff and I can handle the kids, but you've got my best hand with you, and I need Troy to meet me in the canyons tomorrow evening to help with the horses."

Miriam's voice cut off abruptly as she waited, not realizing she hadn't actually asked Jake for anything. Jake looked back over his shoulder at the quickly forming heap of empty bottles and grimaced slightly.

"I'll tell you what." Jake said with a dark scowl at the boisterous cowboys. "We're finished with the cattle, so tomorrow I'll send Derek and Carter down with the trucks, and both Troy and I will come help with the horses. You don't need to worry. We will be there by afternoon or early evening. Okay?"

Miriam's relieved laughter drifted through static into Jake's ears as she sighed and thanked him before giving him details and then hanging up. Jake closed the cover of his phone and slid it back into his pocket. Picking up the scattered remnants of the fractured tree around him, Jake joined the others with the firewood, hoping the beer would take the sting off the fresh distribution of work.

Derek and Carter would not be happy about returning to the ranch to unload without the other two, but Jake didn't trust Carter with Miriam's group. Teen-agers meant teen-age girls, and, drunk or sober, the rough twenty-two year old had a special affinity for teen-age girls. *No.* thought Jake with a slight shake of his head, *I can risk Carter's wrath over being loaded down with the cattle. I can't send him with Troy.*

Jake didn't like Carter. He was the kind of guy who got more confident and stupid when he was drinking. He was also the kind of guy who got more mean and angry when he wasn't. Jake kindled the fire as the men lounged on their saddles laid around the fire, all of them glassy-eyed and cheerful from the beer. Jake lay b ack against the soft leather of his saddle and pulled his hat down over his eyes. He would tell them tomorrow; they wouldn't even remember if he explained it tonight.

Chapter Four

"Jake?" Cassie wondered as she sat perched on a wide, flat boulder above the rushing water of the silver creek wash. When she had asked Miriam for the names of the hostlers who were caring for the horses, Miriam told her they were Jake and Troy.

She'd only worked for The Rocking J for a few weeks, and the names of most of her new coworkers were still hazy in her memory. Troy, she could picture. He was the only one she trusted to care for Jackpot, her sorrel mare. Troy Barnes was gently, straightforward, and firm with the animals as well as their clients. She didn't think she had met Jake yet, and it made her a little nervous.

After rubbing the mare down and picketing her to graze, Cassie told one of the other counselors to let Troy or Jake know that she was going to the river with the blind group. The quiet pool further up the bank was the group's destination, but here, where the water tumbled like socks in a dryer, Cassie relaxed as she listened to the voice of the rapids laughing along with the evening wind. The smell of horses, camp fire, and damp greenery hung around her face like a misty veil in the crisp air.

She did not expect Lindley to smell or sound that different from Albuquerque. The creosote and cactus, pinion and sage were mingled with the echoes of windy canyons and rolling dunes; in her last home, the ranch wasn't near any mountains. The program she had worked for in New Mexico was on a Natchez Indian reservation. The heat, the horses, and the desert sand held no smell of rich earth, rushing water, or towering trees. Her brief stint with The Rocking J had brought a new world to her mind, and a soothing balm to her soul. Her heart belonged in Albuquerque, but her soul needed this new location to heal.

Leaving there had felt like tearing a part of her away, like an old scab that was ready to allow for new skin. Her other jobs had been good ones, but her last one had been her opportunity to live independently, find her limits, fall in love, and fall apart, too.

Lindley was fresh, new, and needing to be explored. There wasn't much she could picture in her mind yet; she needed to feel out the canyons, farmlands, and most importantly the people. Her lack of confidence in that area frightened her, and put other people ill at ease sometimes, but Albuquerque had taught her the world was a nastier place than she'd expected. She had been too trusting, too naive; she would not make that mistake again.

Cassie shook her head to keep herself from picturing the reasons she'd lost her naiveté. Here in the roar of the waterfall she did not want to be haunted by them again. She focused on the smells and sounds floating all around her.

The distant laughter of the teen-agers splashing in the water up the creek stiffened her back slightly until she remembered Jana had taken the group to the railed portion of the bank to teach them to use their ears and senses to locate direction and sound.

The exercises on horseback this afternoon had left her exhausted, and the calming brush of the breeze mixed with the soothing sound of water would heal more than just her nervousness. A scuffle of footsteps and a deep male voice collided loudly at the top of the river bank behind her. Cassie spun toward the bank in surprise. She had been so lost in her reflections of the day, the two voices on the dirt road beyond her soaking spot had intruded without warning.

"It's all right, honey," a deep voice drawled. "Just hold tight to me and I'll get you to the riverside."

A nervous twitter of fear-filled laughter was drowned in the scuffling of gravel, and a young woman's voice sharpening in Cassie's ears. "I think I should wait for Cassie or Jana. I never should have tried to come on my own."

Kirstie Scott, the seventeen-year-old rodeo princess from Reno, was lost and frightened on the bank of the river above Cassie's perch. Last summer, Kirstie had been thrown from her mount, and the frightened animal had kicked her in the head. The traumatic head injury had detached both of her retinas. Surgery had been unsuccessful, and the formerly confident young woman was now trying to learn independence and freedom in a world that held only flashes of light and utter darkness for her.

"Kirstie!" Cassie shouted scrambling off her rock and groping for the slick rocky wall of the gorge behind her. The deep stone hedge and the rush of water over the broken falls tossed the sound back into Cassie's parched mouth as panic now found her as well.

"Trust me, sweetie," the dark, sloppy voice slurred again, and Cassie caught the scent of beer mixed in with the smell of cow and leather.

That's not Troy, Cassie thought, knowing she didn't recognize the male voice. She did, however, identify the smell and the sound of his inebriation, and her heart screamed its protest painfully into her muscles straining for the top of the gorge. Cassie climbed more desperately toward the lip of the steep rock wall focusing on locating hand and footholds.

"Please," Kristie's voice begged the swell of unfallen tears heavy in the sound. "Where are we?"

"Don't worry, baby," came the awful crooning, "You're with me. I'll show you everything you need to see." Cassie scowled and wanted to scream out for help when the drunken charms were extinguished by another deep voice. Cassie heard the brash tone from the other side of the gravel road at the top of the bank

"Carter," a sharp growl interrupted the footsteps above her head, and Cassie paused to listen. "Unless this young lady is looking for the cattle truck, you are in the wrong place with the wrong intentions." A small gasp of relief floated on the breeze, and Cassie sank to the rocky face of the steep incline.

"Get lost, Casanova," the drunken voice hissed sharply. "I don't work for you." Cassie's ears perked again.

"Casanova?" she whispered into the breeze. Was that why she had thought the rescuing words of the other man had seemed some how familiar? Jake Caswell was intervening on behalf of this frightened girl? New panic sparked in Cassie's heart as she wondered if Kirstie had gone from the frying pan into the fire. Jake's voice drifted stiff and stern this time, and Cassie released her grip on the rock now clenched in her fist.

"You don't work for me, Carter," he affirmed, his voice drawing nearer to the river. "And I'll make sure you never work in this county again, if you don't let go of that girl."

"I was just helping the girl find her guides." Carter spat defensively, and Cassie heard Kirstie's soft crying suddenly muffled against someone's shoulder.

"She doesn't want your idea of help, and neither do any of the girls in camp tonight, or any other night. You take those cattle back to the ranch, and I will forget to mention this to my father. If that's not motivation enough for you to leave, then worry about how lucky you are going to get at Mcgoo's tomorrow night if you force me to break your nose this far from a hospital."

"Anytime, Jake. Anywhere." Carter spit menacingly.

Jana's voice was drifting up the road toward Cassie's perch on the edge of the gulch, and she continued to pick her way to the top of the gulley climbing from the edge just as she heard the sounds of crowded footsteps and voices.

"Jana!" Cassie huffed, clamoring onto the dusty road and stumbling toward the group now gathered around Kirstie. Confused at the unseen scene before her, Cassie heard the panicked girl, the angry men disappearing around a distant grove of Aspen trees, and her own footsteps emerging from the edge of the wash.

"Jana," Cassie called again, holding her hand to grab Jana. "Is she all right? Did he hurt her? Did Jake get here in time?" The furious questions spilled from Cassie like the water in the creek far below.

Jana's voice sounded confused as Cassie pictured Jana holding Kirstie against her side, sputtering at the sudden appearance of her friend.

"I don't . . . I think she's . . . Cassie, what? Where did Jake come from? What happened?"

Cassie shook her head and started trying to calm the rest of the frantically confused blind kids.

"I don't know," she said quietly, holding the hands of some of the younger girls. "Let's get them back to camp, and then I need to find Troy."

*

The group moved slowly down the road to the campground, but with familiar sounds and smells wafting toward them, their fear subsided, and tears and trauma were forgotten in favor of hot food and a roaring campfire. Cassie sank to the bench of a concrete picnic table after serving and settling the exhausted teens. She thought for sure she would be fighting her eyelids at this point, but instead, she found her ears perked into the encroaching darkness for the sound of . . . Jake? Troy? She didn't care just as long as it was someone with an explanation.

Without having seen anything, only having heard the words from the top of the cliff, Cassie's imagination was straining not to go wild with speculation. She shivered against the damp night air. Kirstie had told her that she had made her way up the dirt road using the gravel under her feet to keep her near the high side of the river bank. The hollow of the gulch had provided an echo of the rushing water. Kirstie had done pretty well until she became overconfident. She'd finally realized she was still on the road, but the rushing sounds of wind and water had disoriented her, and she was confused about how close she was to the ledge that dropped into the wash.

The roar of a cattle truck had sent Kirstie off the road in terror. Carter had offered his help in locating the rest of the group with her, telling her that he was here to help Troy and would be more than happy to lead her the rest of the way to the river. It wasn't until Kirstie had noticed that he seemed to be trying to lead her *off* the road that she had gotten nervous.

Cassie shook her head to subdue her imagination once more. Kirstie felt a little foolish now, believing that she had overreacted to Carter's attempt at helping her.

"It was my fault, Cassie," she had said. "I get scared so easy, he probably thinks I'm crazy and I think I got him in trouble with his boss. That other guy was pretty mad, and I was just scared because I'm a bad blind person."

Cassie had been impressed with the girl's courage; she was making great progress from the nearly catatonic girl who had arrived at The Rocking J earlier in the week. Their long afternoons on the horse and Cassie's never-ending patience with Kirstie's ever-resurfacing fears had given way to the strength she had needed to walk the road alone.

Kirstie had started to cry again, and Cassie held her until the tears subsided.

"Kirstie," Cassie had said firmly. "The best sense you have right now is your sixth sense. You trusted your instincts and didn't go further than you should have with someone your heart told you not to trust. You may never have proof that you were not safe, but it can't matter." Cassie gingerly reached and wiped Kirstie's tears. "Those feelings have to be trusted and listened to. Eventually you'll learn who you can trust with what, but until then, trust your instincts."

Cassie's thoughts broke from Kirstie as she heard a low whisper from the edge of the dying fire and recognized Troy's voice.

Troy Barnes had been Miriam's right hand man since the inception of the program. He was a quiet, solid worker. He was good with animals, but awkward with people. Cassie got the feeling he was more comfortable with horses and campfires. She reluctantly stood from the bench and made her way toward the low voices, knowing that her few weeks with The Rocking J were going to make Troy's lack of verbal skills even more pronounced in her presence, but she had to find out more about these men.

Cassie sat silently beside Troy as he finished his accounting of the horses to Miriam, leaning back away from the heat of the dancing flames as she waited her turn.

"Where's Jake gone to?" she asked, without mincing words.

"He left with Carter," Troy answered, hesitantly.

Cassie spoke into the darkness of the night. "Who is this Carter?"

"He's a local boy. He hires on with a few places to take up the slack."

Cassie nodded her head slightly and pressed on. "What was he doing here today?"

"Carter wasn't supposed to be here. He hired on with Caswell Farms to help with the spring round up. Jake told him to take the last of the cattle back down to the valley with Derek Parker, another guy who works for Caswells." Cassie was expecting more, but when Troy was silent except for the uncomfortable shuffling of his feet, Cassie pressed on.

"How did he end up on the road by Silver Creek?"

"Look, Miss Taylor," Troy hesitated, his hands sounding busy with the fire. "I can appreciate you looking out for your job and these kids, but Carter is just a kid himself. He drinks too much, and he's got a mean streak, but he wouldn't have hurt that girl today, and I don't think I'm the right guy to be trying to convince you not to be suspicious."

Cassie stood and stepped toward the stoic man's voice, meeting him with crossed arms and pursed lips. "Why?" she asked. "Why aren't you the man to convince me that Carter, or Jake for that matter, should be trusted?"

"That's just it. This wasn't about your girl or what I think of Carter Langdon. Carter doesn't like Jake, and when Jake ordered him to take the cattle back down the mountain while he and I came to help Miriam, Carter took that as a direct invitation to come."

Cassie stepped beside him. "What's Carter's problem with Jake? Is he too much competition for the same women?"

Troy laughed a bark of humorless mirth. "More like the fact that there is no competition. Carter is so green with envy, he spits pea soup. Jake is the only guy around here with even the possibility of a life beyond Lindley. Carter can't stand it that Jake could be somewhere else having a life and still comes back here."

"I thought Jake has a life somewhere else?"

"Yeah, he does. He's got it all. Hollywood, money, women, the ranch, family, friends, everything, but Jake is a man torn between two worlds, and it drives Carter crazy. He would sell his right hand to have even a part of what Jake has, so every chance he gets he lets Jake know he's waiting to pull him down if he can."

"So Carter figured there was something here Jake wanted, and if Jake told him to go the other direction he had better come take whatever Jake was keeping from him?"

The sound of Troy's mumbled agreement made Cassie wonder if he was the right person to talk to about this. His opinions were bordering on worship of Jake, and he was rather noncommittal as far as Carter was concerned.

Before her worries and the night could steal any more energy from her tired legs, Cassie sat down beside the fire. "What did Jake have here that Carter wanted?"

Troy made an exasperated sound in his throat, then stepped away from Cassie. "Nothing. Jake came to help Mrs. Sorenson, that's all. Just because Jake can get whatever he wants doesn't mean he's out to take advantage of everyone."

Cassie tilted her head skeptically. "Then why isn't he here helping?"

"Because Jake knew the best help he would be to me and The Rocking J was for him to get Carter out of here."

"I'm sorry, Troy. I don't know Jake or Carter, and in my world, trust is earned. Carter isn't getting far in that arena and Jake's . . . reputation with the women I've met isn't doing much for him either. I'm not from around here. I'm just trying to figure out this whole mess before someone gets hurt."

Cassie heard Troy throw something onto the fire, before walking away from her. "It's only when you're afraid to get hurt that you won't take a chance on trust, Miss Taylor."

Chapter Five

"Jake." Gary Burke's voice draped itself like silk over Jake's tired mind. "Where you been? Universal is pounding down my door to find out if you're available for fall shooting in New Zealand. They've got the horses from the outlands for only three months, and they need to know if you're on board for the shoot."

Jake tossed his sweat-stained Stetson onto the bed and then stripped off his dirty clothes. Tossing his dusty shirt and jeans into a basket across the room, Jake spoke loud enough for his speaker phone to pick up his voice. "September's okay," he said, grabbing a towel and picking up the phone. "But I'm here until late August to start the new alfalfa crop."

"Jake, why do you waste your time in that godforsaken desert? The women can't be that pretty."

Jake laughed, rolling his eyes at Gary. He could almost see the look on his agent's face even from the other side of the high Sierra peaks looming between them. "Women are the same everywhere. I go where the work is, here, New Zealand. doesn't really matter," he said with a shrug in his voice. "So book me a flight in September, and I'll talk to you later."

Jake threw the phone back on his bed. Stretching his sore muscles, he looked in the mirror, noticing the faint tan line starting to form at his throat and biceps. The ripple of muscle and sinew beneath his tan took on a hard-chiseled edge in the fading light, and Jake admired the way his body had grown lean and sculpted under the labors of the ranch. His eyes unconsciously drifted back to the imperfection of the quickly forming farmer's tan and he frowned.. Tomorrow when he went out to dam the creek and take Heidi swimming in the reservoir, he'd need to work bare-chested to even out his skin tone. He tossed his dark hair back from his brow and noticed the dark circles under his eyes. He'd only slept a few hours last night after unloading the cattle and stabling the horses. Friday had slipped beyond the hot afternoon sun, and Jake longed for a hot shower and the relief of his bed. His phone played its song and he walked back to glance at caller I.D. before answering it.

"Hey, Lilly."

"Hi, Jake. Are you going to Mcgoo's tonight?"

Jake sank onto his back on the bed, looking up at the ceiling. "Not tonight, Lil. I've been sleeping on the ground for a week, and I've got to get some rest."

A pouting harrumph made Jake grin widely as he pictured the pretty face of the dark-haired girl. Lilly was a cross between a Cherokee temptress and a Polynesian princess. Her skin was like warm brown sugar, her hair like satin dark chocolate. Yummy was always the word that came to Jake's mind when he kissed her. Lilly was like him though, a part-time player at Mcgoo's.

They had hooked up two summers back with the understanding they were both just looking for a way out of the boredom in a small town. Her dad was a handler with a California beef buyer, and he only came to Lindley for a few months during the summer to hand pick the best of the summer slaughter. Lilly's mom spent summers in Mexico with her family, and Lilly hated the lack of privacy in a busy hacienda so she came north with her dad. Jake and Lilly were . . . friends. Friends with privileges; Jake smiled to hold back laughter.

She would not suffer for his lack of appearance at Mcgoo's tonight, and they both knew it. Lilly liked to have Jake around to help her ditch the cowboys she didn't like, and she was his best Natalie Harper deterrent, but Jake didn't need Lilly's distraction keeping him from sleep tonight.

"Do me a favor, Lil," he said, sitting back up and yawning.

"Stay away from Carter Langdon tonight, will ya? He's in a bad mood, and I don't want him taking it out on you."

Lilly harrumphed again, and Jake almost changed his mind. "Carter's easy," she assured, "You avoid him until he's good and drunk, then you buy him a round of Jack Daniels and take away his keys. He'll sleep it off in his truck."

"I know you can handle him, but I had a problem with him on the way down last night and tonight he's coaxing a grudge. J.D. will only nurse him into a criminal, so no games tonight. Okay?"

"Fine," Lilly pouted once more, "Ruin all my fun, but you will be dealing with Natalie alone. Her cousin Zach is here from Stanford, and I'm seriously considering letting him fall in love with me at her party tomorrow night."

Jake laughed out loud now, shaking his head at her easy joking. "He doesn't stand a chance, Lilly. Just let me know which night you decide to let him down easy."

Jake hung up and blew out a deep breath. "What are you doing?" he asked out loud to no one. "Sleeping," he answered himself. "That's what you should be doing."

Friday night slipped thankfully into dreamless sleep and the rest of his weekend remained contentedly quiet. The time passed quickly as Jake looked forward to the days he would spend in the mountains. It was one week later when he found himself surrounded by the lights and noises of Mcgoo's once more.

*

Setting his icy glass down on the edge of the round table in the far corner of the bar, Jake sank into the chair beneath him. *Mcgoo's is chaos tonight,* he thought, looking around at the pressing throngs of people. It was the first night of the summer rodeo series and the Pro-Bull Riders were in town. The small rural area made all its tourist revenue during the rodeo series, and Jake had been signing autographs with the stars of the PBR since the doors of Mcgoo's had opened at eight.

As the crowd of drunken cowboys and girls surged, Jake pressed deeper into the shadows. Everyone and their cousin, literally, were here tonight. Jake relaxed now, in the shadowed corner, letting a breeze from the bar's fan waft over his face. This dark corner had been good company these past few weeks. Tonight it would do him even better thanks to the thickening of the crowd. Picking up his sweating glass, he caught sight of a tall half-empty glass of lemonade sitting on a paper coaster in the center of the table.

He pulled back his hand from the occupied surface as if it were a boiling candle against his skin. A deep frown creased his mouth as he tried to look past the crowded bodies to see if the auburn-haired girl with the icy blue eyes was nearby.

As Jake turned toward the swinging doors of the exit, the sound of dragging chair legs scuffled beside him. Troy Barnes's voice brought Jake's gaze back to the room.

"It's wild in here tonight, Cassie," Troy shouted at the girl now occupying the chair next to Jake. "Will you be all right if I leave you here for a second?" Jake watched the quick smile dance across Cassie's lips as she looked at Troy and nodded. Troy stood straight and noticed Jake sitting in the back corner.

He grimaced slightly at Jake and nodded toward Cassie mouthing, "Watch her."

Jake frowned but nodded back as Troy melted back into the sea of bodies and light.

This was the last girl Jake wanted to watch tonight. He already had a half-dozen phone numbers and e-mail addresses. He wasn't looking to waste opportunity and energy on this girl. He took a deep breath and folded his arms across his chest as she turned in her chair and reached for her lemonade.

"I'm guessing that Troy's attempt at secrecy means you have been assigned to watch out for me," she said loudly, not looking at

Jake. She stared out into the space in front of her as if he was not there, but he knew she was talking to him.

Leaning forward Jake smiled and said, "I've never seen Troy worried about anybody that doesn't have four legs. Is he your boyfriend?"

Cassie tossed back her hair and laughed, turning to look him in the eye. "No, we work together, and I think he's afraid he'll have to leave the horses to take care of the kids if he loses me in this craziness."

Jake smiled again. "You work at The Rocking J?" he asked, knowing he had either danced with or kissed every one of Miriam's female staff.

"For over a month now."

"I've never seen you around."

Jake was suddenly intrigued that he hadn't noticed Cassie after their last encounter. She had been less than six miles from his ranch.

"You mean since the last time we shared this table?" she asked with a bitter smile. She turned her eyes back to her glass, keeping her head down and her hair between them.

Jake nodded before realizing with her curtain of auburn strands between them she could not see the response. "I thought maybe you hadn't recognized me," he said with a slow shake of his dark hair. He pushed the tangled curls from off his forehead and offered her one of his signature smiles. She didn't look up at him but lifted her head to focus into the distance again.

"From what I have heard about you," she said turning toward him. "You are easy to recognize."

Jake grinned and ran his hands through his hair with a tilt of his chin and a silken quality to his voice. "You've been asking about me?"

Cassie shook her head and frowned at him. "No Jake, but there are a lot of people around here who seem to see something in you that, for the life of me, I just don't see."

He was the recipient of one of her icy glares, and she turned her back on him for the second time since he had met her.

Jake picked up his drink, feeling suddenly trapped with this girl. "Maybe that just means you should have your eyes checked."

Cassie shook her head helplessly, and then laughed at him. "Maybe I just see through the masks most people can't see through. Maybe if you really *were* the man you pretend to be instead of just *looking* like him, I wouldn't need to see anything at all."

Jake's expression became stony as she turned on him again, her pale blue eyes seeming to look right through him. He suddenly felt a sharp pang of fear strike him in the chest. Her fathomless eyes were piercing, as if she really could see past the charm, the silken words, and the magic of his deep blue eyes. Looking at her now, he believed her, she really couldn't see it.

Jake pushed his chair back into the corner and stood, holding a hand out to her. "Come dance with me, Cassie," he said the gruff quiet cowboy drawl sure to convince her she was wrong about him. "I think you should spend more than a couple of minutes judging me before you know what kind of a man I am."

Cassie frowned and then looked as if she might turn her back on him again. "All right, Jake," she agreed putting her hand out and forcing him to reach out and take it. "If you really think my sight problems can be cleared up after one dance, then I have two rules."

As she stood, Jake shoved her chair aside and began winding toward the floor to break through the crowd. Cassie stood still, her feet planted, and he dropped her hand at her defiance.

"Rules?" he said, coming back toward her. Crossing his arms over his chest, he met her eyes with his best repentant little boy smile, trying to soften her unfaltering gaze. She looked through him again, not even a flick of her lip or twitch of her cheek giving her away.

Jake took a broken breath, "Okay, tell me the rules."

Cassie grimaced now, as she was shoved and jostled by the

pressing crowd. A panicked glint caught in her deep eyes, and Jake felt its flash of fear along with her. He stepped toward her placing his hands at her elbows to steady her as she held up one finger. "First, you hold onto me until we get on the dance floor. You can't get tired of me halfway across the floor and just walk off."

Jake grinned; she was not as unaffected by him as she pretended to be.

"Second, you take me back to the same chair I was just sitting in when it's over."

Jake's face crumpled in confusion. "That's it?" he asked, taking her hand and uncrossing her arms. "No bloodletting or fight to the death with an alligator? Just take you on and off the floor?"

Cassie nodded her head as he looked back at her over his shoulder. "That's all I need from you," she murmured.

Jake found an open place on the dance floor and pulled her into his arms.

"Deal," he said, letting his voice drop low and gruff, pressing his mouth against her ear.

She pulled back from him, making sure she was only touching him with the palms of her hands. Jake looked at her, stupefied.

"I feel like I'm dancing with my grandmother," he complained putting his hand on her back and pushing her toward him. "Except my grandma stands closer to me than this."

Cassie stiffened in his hold and tilted her head up at him. "Don't tell me you use this cowboy charm even on your poor grandmother."

Jake threw his head back and laughed. "You know you're a lot of fun when you're not trying so hard to dislike me."

Cassie narrowed her eyes at him as he pressed them into the path of another couple to close the space they had between them.

"Who says I even have to try?" she said, straightening her arms and stepping back into a small space between couples.

Jake pulled her firmly from the narrow space with fresh fervor, and she stumbled against him, finally, as he wrapped both arms around her waist. She glared at him again, and then turned her face away to stare across the crowded pressing bodies all around. A lock of her hair had fallen into her eyes, and Jake moved his arm from her waist to free it from her lashes, knowing the tender gesture had melted more than one hard heart. With the release of his hold, Cassie backed away from him once again, shaking the hair from her lashes and planting her feet on the floor in front of him.

"The song's over, Jake," she said firmly. "My chair?"

She was still holding on to his arm and her mixed messages only pricked his competitive nature to grin at her. "You said when we were done, I should take you back." He pulled her stiffly into his arms again. "I'm not done."

The music had slowed, and Jake felt her surrender. He held her firmly, tenderly, and she relaxed her death grip on his hand and let him hold her against his body as the dancers now barely moved in response to the romantic ballad.

Cassie sighed and looked up at him. "This is a waste of a good excuse to get some beautiful girl out here to make out with you."

Jake laughed again, still surprised at how blunt she was. He could feel the defiance slipping out of her, but it was being replaced with a frantic energy, like a wild mustang that will let you touch its nose and slide your hand along his flanks, but the instant he feels pressure on his back he runs.

"Relax, Cassie," Jake said, his voice a deep sultry whisper again. "I don't bite."

Cassie stiffened in response to the honey softness of his verbal caress. "It's not your teeth I should be watching out for," she grumbled quietly, leaning away from him.

Jake kept her firmly wrapped in his arms and danced them both across the floor, before the song had ended. "See," he said. "There's more to me than disagreements in dark corners."

Cassie shook her head, backing away from his hold on her.

"That's just it. If that was more . . . then I've already seen more than enough."

She turned her back on him and felt her way through the throngs of people and dim atmosphere to the wall, disappearing into the crowd.

Chapter Six

"Jake Caswell, that arrogant, manipulative snake!" Cassie's mind fumed the most powerful pointed names she could imagine, but she didn't actually know very many, and the blinding fury in her heart blocked out rational thought.

She felt the whisper of wind breezing through the swinging doors and she pushed them out, and past too many bodies. She followed the tracer of hot panic in her heart until she bumped against a vehicle and paused to catch her breath. *I hope you're happy now, Troy.* She fumed all over again. *I tried.*

Cassie took in the crispness of the night. How many nights had she danced with Dylan? She remembered the way it felt to be in his arms, to feel his breath in her ear. Jake had been so familiar, too familiar, and that acid falseness had drizzled from his lips just as sweetly. Cassie ground her teeth until the sound made her wince away from those pictures. Instead she cleared her mind and let the atmosphere around her trickle down to quiet her troubled heart and mind as she became awash in the night. The melodic hum of crickets mingled with the distant roar of the river up the canyon. Muted voices and music humming in staccato against the breath of the evening greeted her ears; the smell of moss, pine, sage, and sand drifted past her nose.

"Cassie?" Troy's voice broke her silent reverie. "Are you okay? Jake said he lost you in the crowd. Are you lost?"

"No, Troy, not lost. I left when Jake was more concerned with showing off than he was with anything or anyone else."

Troy chuckled under his breath, and Cassie felt him take her elbow. "Are you sure? Do you know where you are?"

"I know exactly where I am. I am misplaced somewhere in a parking lot."

"Misplaced, huh? Not lost?"

"After twenty years of doing this Troy, do you really think I would get lost in a parking lot?"

Chapter Seven

"Jake." Debra Caswell's voice brought him to full awareness now sitting up in bed and rubbing his eyes.

"Mom?" he groaned falling back into his pillow and pulling it over his head.

Debra stood with her arms crossed and her lips pursed, tapping her foot against the footboard of his bed until the slight vibrations annoyed him into looking up at her.

"Jake Caswell, it's two thirty in the afternoon, and you have been asleep all day."

Jake sat back up, panic clearing the sleep from his mind.

"Dad and Derek took care of your chores, and tended the horses before they left for Los Angeles with Armando Pinion, but I need your help now."

Jake nodded wordlessly, focusing on his mother's words and fighting a return of sleep. Debra stepped back from his bed, throwing a dirty look at the pile of napkins and coasters still on the dresser from the night before. It was actually this morning, he thought, as he rotated on the bed to swing his long legs over the side to the floor. Resting his throbbing skull in his hands, propped on his knees, Jake blocked out the blaring sun breaking through the window, trying to ignore his mother's fussing about the room.

"You don't have any of the girls who belong to those phone numbers stashed in here with you somewhere, do you?" Debra said, frowning and glancing around Jake's chaotic room. Dirty boots and blue jeans hid the floor from view and Debra pushed a mound aside to look under his bed. "I know you're an adult and everything," her voice was muffled by the dark recess of the under side of his mattress, "but if you're going to pick up girls, don't bring them back here, please." Debra's long dark hair popped up from below the edge of the bed and Jake frowned disapprovingly. "Don't give me that face, Jake. I know what girls who put their phone numbers on cocktail napkins are after."

Jake did his best to look shocked and horrified at his mother's too—knowing comments. "Mom," he gasped in mock disdain. "I am not that kind of guy, and my mama didn't raise me like that."

Debra Caswell rolled her eyes, picking up one of his pillows and batting him in the face with it.

"Get dressed." She commanded, not able to hold back her own good natured smile. "I need you to go to The Rocking J and pick up Heidi."

Jake nodded and rubbed his yawning jaw.

As he stood and began stumbling toward his bedroom door, his mother began throwing the dirty clothes into the mostly empty basket, and a memory of pale blue eyes suddenly filled his mind. He paused briefly, his hand on the open door.

"Have you met Miriam's new counselor?" he asked as his mother pushed the basket in front of her with her foot.

She paused, a look of concentration on her face, deepening the lines around her eyes and mouth.

"I don't think so," she said with a shrug, pushing past Jake into the hallway.

He followed her down the hall until he stood in front of the bathroom and she was at the top of the stairs. Bending down to pick up the basket, she lifted it to one hip and then turned to grin at her handsome son in the doorway.

"I should be asking you. I didn't think there was a girl within a thousand miles of here you haven't had track you down."

"What makes you think the new counselor is a girl?" he asked stepping into the bathroom and turning on the shower to warm it up.

"Heidi works with her and Applesauce twice a week." Debra yelled to be heard over the sound of the shower.

Jake pulled his wet hand out from under the nozzle and popped his head around the partially opened door. "Heidi works with her?" he said trying not to let his mother see the glint in his eye.

"Twice a week," Debra repeated as she descended the staircase.

Jake grinned at his mother's disappearing form. So she wasn't softening up to him at the bar. Maybe she just didn't like pick ups in bars. Jake closed the bathroom door and got into the shower, thoughts forming with clarity as the hot water washed away his drowsiness. She worked with his sister and that would give him the chance to break that icy exterior. He'd never known a female that could resist him for too long.

"You had better get this one," he said to himself as he soaped his hair and grinned wickedly. "Casanova is a name you earned, and this girl is ruining it." He stepped farther into the spray of hot water, rinsing as quickly as he could. The summer had just gotten started, and he was bored already. This would be a good game to stir things up a little, and keep him distracted from his growing unease.

Jake left the shower and dressed quickly but carefully. It was Sunday afternoon; he could show up at the horse ranch dressed as if he hadn't been working the cattle, but he traded his leather pants for black jeans at the last minute. Cassie had seen those at the club the first time he'd run into her, and, though he was trying to break her icy façade, she seemed to be less impressed with his Hollywood look than other girls, so he opted for his rough-and-rugged look. He left the first three buttons of his white shirt unbuttoned, his tawny skin catching the rays of the afternoon sun and the thin layer of dark whisker across his jaw like dark velvet against his strong features. He escaped the ranch house without his mother coming out of the laundry room, shouting through the kitchen door that he was going to pick up Heidi.

*

Jake listened to his messages as he drove toward The Rocking J. He skipped the three that Natalie had left him, instead checking Facebook and Twitter for comments from the new crowd of fans he had picked up at the rodeo. Tonight was the final show and the bull rides. Lilly preferred the Bronco riders, but she would want to go with him to the V.I.P. section of the stands. He skipped past Gary's message with his agenda for New Zealand, listening to Lilly's silken voice.

"You're on your own tonight, Jake," Lilly's message said without even a greeting. "I'm going back to California with my dad." Jake thought he could almost hear a choked sob break her voice as she paused; his heart took a dive. "I'm sick and tired of playing with little boys." There was another pause, and Lil's breath rang over the recording. "I can't waste . . . I'm going back. Take care." Jake dropped the phone on the passenger seat next to him, squinting into the bright afternoon blare. He couldn't tell if she was mad at him or at something that had happened last night. When he had left Mcgoo's at 2 a.m., she had been knee-deep in rodeo cowboys and had assured him he could go.

After Cassie had stormed out, and he had gotten a good chewing from Troy for losing her, Jake had been in a sour mood. Even the fireworks had done nothing but remind him of that white flash of fury in Cassie's eyes, and his frustration with her had driven him home, alone. Jake grimaced again, picking up his phone from the seat next to him, and dialing Lilly's number, only managing to get her voicemail.

"Hey, Lil," he said attempting to sound more nonchalant than he felt. "What's the deal? You bailing on me? Did you end up falling for Zach Harper after all? Call me, okay?"

Jake tossed the phone onto the passenger seat of his car again, trying to shake Lilly's distress from his mind. Something in the sound of her voice poked guiltily at him, and he wanted it to stop.

As the white rail fence of The Rocking J came into sight, he focused more fiercely on his current challenge, pushing his unease to the back of his mind and only casually noting that, except for the ten or so weeks he and Lilly hooked up in the summer and a couple of times a year on Facebook, they didn't really have a relationship and thus far, she might be his best friend.

The silver Mitsubishi came to a stop in a cloud of dusty gravel in front of Miriam Sorenson's farm house. Through the screen door he could see movement in the kitchen and heard Miriam's voice, but he didn't hear Heidi's.

Climbing from the car, he vaulted the porch steps and knocked gently on the door before swinging it open and poking his head through. "It's Jake," he called out, before entering the warm kitchen, passing first through the wide screened porch that served as the dining hall for the weekend groups. Stepping up to the hardwood floors, Jake threw a half smile to the women who were sitting around a pine table, eating sandwiches and drinking lemonade. Miriam sat at the end, her dark hair sticking to her moist forehead. Jana Pembrooke and Lacey Gibson sat at either side of her and looked up as Jake sauntered through the door. Lacey grinned at him, her brown eyes inspecting every feature and her lips widening at his smile. Jana just stared. He had met Jana a bunch of times, but whenever he tried polite conversation or even just looked at her, the girl was practically comatose.

"Jake," Lacey said pulling out the chair beside her at the table and patting the seat. "Come have lunch with us. You look good enough to eat." Lacey jumped in her chair a little, and Jake saw Jana's mouth drop in blatant embarrassment at the girl's comment. It quickly became obvious to Jake that Miriam had kicked Lacey under the table, and Jana had felt the jolt of it as well.

Jake smiled crookedly, shoving his hands into the pockets of his jeans and watching the looks pass between the three girls.

"I'd love to have lunch with three such beautiful ladies," he drawled casually, "but one of the Caswell women has sent me and the other is expecting a ride home, so my lunch hour doesn't belong to me." A new blush of scarlet crossed Jana's cheeks, and Jake smiled at her to ensure it would remain. "Can you tell me where to find Heidi?"

Lacey flashed him another tempestuous look and started to rise from her seat when Miriam placed a hand over hers and stood herself. "Lacey, you and Jana finish up in here, and I'll take Jake to the barn."

Jake grinned again as the blond girl's face fell in disappointment, and Miriam squashed it with a warning glance.

"Come on, Jake," Miriam said, taking him by the arm and hustling him out the door.

She didn't give Lacey or the still-silent Jana the chance to protest. Waiting for the screen door to slam before pinching his arm, Miriam scolded, "Jake Caswell, you know those girls will be useless to me for the rest of the day. The least you could do when you come is show up *after* a round up or a day repairing fences." Jake held back a chuckle as Miriam looked back at the screen door to the kitchen. "You show up here looking like . . . that." She punctuated the word with a flourish of her hand toward him. "And I'll be lucky if I can get you off my land without one of my girls stowed away in the trunk of your car."

"I'll try and remember," he said faking a serious tone. "Hot, sweaty, and filthy. And I'm welcome."

Miriam looked up at him with a sideways glance and a grin on her face. "That probably wouldn't be any better," she said with a shake of her head and a failing frown. "We'll just have to learn to keep the girls out in the paddock when you come to pick up Heidi."

He tried to look apologetic as they rounded the corner of the barn, and Miriam stopped, pointing toward the corrals. "She's just finishing up with Applesauce and Cassie. You'll see them on the other side of the doors."

Jake smiled again and lifted an eyebrow questioningly, "Cassie? Aren't you worried about Cassie being useless for the day? Especially if I'm such a distraction for your girls?"

Miriam turned to head back to the house and pivoted back to look at Jake. "Have you ever met Cassie?" she asked, the edge of something in her question.

"A couple of times at Mcgoo's," he answered keeping his expression blank. Miriam tilted an eyebrow and then shot him a half-hearted smile.

"So . . . then, she gets all befuddled when you're around, too?"

Jake didn't answer with anything except a shrug of his shoulders, and Miriam gave him a watery smile. "I think Cassie will be all right," she said, suddenly brightening and waving him toward the spot she had showed him.

*

Jake watched her return to the big house and then turned toward the barn doors as he heard laughter drifting through the wide opening toward him.

"Showtime, Jake," he murmured as he steadied himself against the sound of Cassie's presence as he walked through the shadowed recesses of the barn. The summer sun was baking the smell of leather, feed, hay, and dirt into a steamy cloud as he passed beneath the loft, and he rushed through it to step into the sunlight. He could see Heidi's long dark hair swaying in the breeze that trickled through the corral as she rubbed her gray mare Applesauce down with a dry cloth.

Heidi loved that horse, despite being generally afraid of the animals. She had become attached to the old mare's warm, dark eyes and velvet muzzle the first time Jake had showed her how to pet it. Jake shook his head at the sight of the ugly beast standing placidly in the hot sun with the two girls. Applesauce wasn't exactly a swaybacked nag, but her coat was mottled gray, like granite that couldn't decide which shade to be. Her back and legs were thick and strong, but the horse paid no mind to speed or destination, preferring to meander like a wandering brook. The placid nature of the old horse convinced Heidi she could be around the gentle animal.

Jake's mustang, Deseo, had been caught and tamed from the wild herd that ran in the deep meadows of the high country, and Heidi was terrified of the blond stallion. Deseo snorted like a wild bull and was given to unannounced mad dashes even under Jake's firm hand. But Jake loved the horse's unquenchable spirit and the freedom he felt riding bareback through the stands of aspens climbing the slopes of the lower Sierras.

His dad had given Applesauce to Miriam, hoping the methodical plod of the old mare would help Heidi learn at least to walk the exercise ring on her back. Both Heidi and the mare had made a lot of progress lately, and Jake suspected Cassie was at least partially responsible. A month ago Heidi hadn't gotten any closer to the horse than the stretch of her fingers toward her silken nose, but now she pulled carrots from her pockets and was letting the horse eat directly out of her hand.

Grinning broadly as he walked quietly to the corral to watch her, Jake saw the trepidation mixed with elation light Heidi's dancing eyes. He was still a few steps back from where Cassie leaned against the side of the rails of the corral, whispering soft words into the horse's ear. A sudden gust of wind blew from behind Jake, and he brushed a tangle of curls back from his forehead, with his fingertips, letting the cool touch of the slight wind soften the sun's glare.

Cassie suddenly stiffened her back and stood straight, pulling back from Applesauce and holding her hand up, palm out toward Jake. In a quiet whisper, he barely heard her warn him to stop.

Jake stood quietly a broad smile across his face; she hadn't even seen him. She had sensed that distraction Miriam had complained to him about earlier, and his expression became smug at her inability to ignore him when he was near.

"Heidi," Jake heard Cassie say softly. "When she's finished, let's let her run back out in the pasture. Your brother is here to get you." Heidi looked up from her scrutiny of Applesauce's lips and teeth in the palm of her hand and noticed Jake, arms crossed over his chest, waiting behind Cassie.

Jake's sudden appearance startled Heidi, and she dropped the remnants of the half eaten carrots to the ground with a shaky smile. "Hi, Yake," she whispered loudly. "Do you see I'm feeding the horse?"

Jake smiled widely at her, and then took two more steps to stand beside Cassie at the rail.

"She's not even scared of me or anything. Cassie says she trusts me, and if I trust her there isn't anything we can't do, even ride . . . fast."

Applesauce finished the carrot in her mouth, and the girl, bright-eyed and eager, pulled back from the horse. Jake shot Cassie a crooked smile; now she would see him truly, not in a bar, not sullen and avoiding Natalie. Just that unmistakable, palpable presence she could not fight.

Heidi moved the rail from the corral behind her to let the horse back into the field, and then turned for approval from Jake.

Jake grinned widely at her, "You are so good with that horse, Heidi. I think you might be ready to come break mustangs in Wyoming with me."

Jake saw his mistake at once, as Heidi turned wild eyed to look at him, fear running rampant in her face.

He meant to encourage her progress, as he put his arm around her and kissed the top of her head. Her brimming eyes and trembling shoulders made it clear he had failed. He was usually so careful with his words, especially where Heidi was concerned. Distracted by his plans for charming Cassie, he hadn't been thinking. Cassie was not charmed, though. Her back stiffened at Heidi's response.

"No, Yake, no," she said pushing away from him. "You said you're not leaving until September, and then the snow will be too deep in Wyoming for riding horses. You promised me, Yake. You promised me."

"I'm sorry," he said over and over again, rubbing her bare arms and looking directly into her overflowing eyes. "You're right. No Wyoming, no mustangs. I'm sorry I said that. Calm down, sweetie, there's no reason to panic. I was being stupid, I'm not going, you're not going. I wasn't thinking."

Heidi buried her head against Jake's chest, and he threw an apologetic smile at Cassie, who stood stone-faced. After Jake had assured Heidi they were not going to Wyoming another hundred times, she wiped her eyes and leaned exhausted against his shoulder. Jake smiled brokenly at Cassie, still trying to get a flicker of something from her unyielding features, but her expression remained unwavering.

"I hope I didn't just set you back," Jake mumbled apologetically. "I really am impressed with how far you have gotten her."

"It's not me, Jake. Heidi is like most people . . . and horses too. She is remarkable when she is partnered with someone . . . or something . . ." Cassie said gesturing toward the pasture, "that she trusts."

Jake made no movement and his mouth fought back another sharp retort, as if Cassie had just accused him of something, but he didn't know what.

Cassie tossed her hair, now copper in the sunlight, over her shoulder and turned her back to them. "You better take her home, Jake. She's had a long day, and I think she needs you to hang onto her for awhile."

Jake nodded, forgetting his ulterior motives for being there. That distant all-seeing look was in her eyes, and this was not the time to try and change her mind about who he was. He needed to reassure Heidi instead.

Chapter Eight

"Jake, what are you doing?" Cassie leaned her back against the corral's railing. She had known Jake was behind her and Heidi before he had appeared. She caught a whiff of the faint hint of his soap and skin, mingled with the smell of the barn as it had drifted on the breeze. Her only concern had been his effect on the horse and Heidi if his sudden presence were to startle either of them. She had not predicted that artificial charm of his would drip from his lips, to bounce back and smack him in the face, though. Heidi was going to be fine, but now whatever Jake's careful appearance had been arranged to accomplish, Heidi had distracted him from his purpose.

Cassie tossed her hair back from her neck, sticky in the burning afternoon sun, finally allowing herself a smile. She listened as Jake talked calmly and smoothly to his little sister. A pang of incredulity bit at her heart. His voice was different when he was sincere. She had heard the difference in the canyon that evening with Kirstie, and she heard it now as Jake talked with his sister as they approached the deeper recesses of the barn. It had been in every word he had said since his arrival. Though it may have backfired on him, he had been truly honest in his appraisal of Heidi's newly developed skills with her horse.

Cassie mentally chastised herself for not intervening after Heidi's misunderstanding. She could have at least encouraged his gentle and appropriate handling of the frantic young girl. With her mind racing, Cassie turned her face toward the sound of his car and grimaced darkly. Fear had never made for good decisions. Why did she have such a tenuous grip on her opinion of a guy who was about as deep as a puddle in the desert?

The depths of his voice poked in her thoughts as she listened to him calmly reassure Heidi. She could tell he was behind the barn and would not assume she could hear him, so she tuned her ears into his charismatic tones.

"Heidi, I'm going to put you in my car. I will tell Miriam we are going, and then we will drive back to the farm, together. I'm not leaving, I am going home too."

Cassie smiled again as he carefully reassured Heidi. He did know how to be real; maybe he was just out of practice with other women.

Chapter Nine

Jake settled Heidi into the passenger side of his car, then strode quickly to the kitchen door of the house. Miriam frowned. "You okay?"

Jake smiled. "We're fine, I just stuck my foot in my mouth with Heidi, and I need to take her home."

Miriam nodded with sudden clarity in her brown eyes, turning back for the dishes. With a half-hearted wave she excused him, and Jake retreated the way he had come in, hoping to avoid any more entanglements. He jogged quickly to his car, slipping into the driver's seat, persuading the ignition to life.

Backing out of the driveway, Jake saw a flash of auburn hair in the rearview mirror, and he watched it dance in the quavering wind. Grimacing as she turned toward the sound of his car, Jake took his eyes from the reflection of her icy glare in the glass. The look on her face was stern and disapproving, and he curled his upper lip in distaste as it prodded his guilt into irritation.

"I'm sorry about that, Heidi," he said under his breath. "I think you and Cassie are doing great with Applesauce. I'm just sorry she had to be there to see me mess everything up."

Heidi had been quiet now that her tears had subsided, and she suddenly turned to stare wide eyed at Jake's unhappy expression.

"Yake," she said, scowling. "You should not talk about the horses, but it doesn't matter if you mess up with Cassie there, too."

"I don't think she likes me very much. I don't like Cassie seeing me mess up. I want her to like me."

Heidi wrinkled her brow, and Jake tried to think of what he had said that would have caused such confusion on her pretty face. "But Yake," she said plaintively, "Cassie can't see anything. She's blind."

Stunned silence filled the car as Jake drove the rest of the way home. Heidi wanted to know why he looked so funny, and why Cassie didn't like him, and why this and why that, but Jake just shook his head, mumbling pacifying responses. His thoughts were numb, but his mind raced to understand what Heidi had said. Maybe she had just meant that Cassie was blind to his charms or good looks or . . . ? Heidi didn't know how to use the word blind figuratively. When she said Cassie was blind, she meant Cassie was physically blind.

Images from the few times she had met him coursed through his memory. Those pale blue eyes, almost haunting, the way she would look out into a room and see . . . nothing. How she could talk to him without looking at him, as if she were focused on someone else in the room. Jake shook his head slightly, and Heidi looked at him.

"Yake, why doesn't Cassie like you? I tell her all the time how nice you are, and how much you work with the cows and the horses, and how I think you should live here with me and mom and dad. She always says I'm lucky to have such a good big brother, but I tell her there is no luck, just genes. We have the same genes."

Jake listened with a halting smile as Heidi babbled beside him like a mountain brook. She had forgotten about the mustangs and was now completely focused on Cassie. She had a million things to say, and she told him all about Cassie. Cassie had come to work for Miriam because she was trained in equine therapy but specialized in mobility and independence for the blind. She was from Danbury, Connecticut, and had been on horseback since she had gone blind when she was four years old. She had gone to Missoula, Montana, for college where she got her psychology and sociology degree and had preferred the heartier Western stock to the blue-blooded horses on the expensive farms of Connecticut. She had lived in New Mexico and Arizona before coming to Lindley to work for Miriam.

"How did she go blind?"

"Her eyes stopped working," Heidi said sleepily. Jake rolled his eyes and smiled at her as they pulled the car up to the ranch house.

"So do you know what made them stop working?"

Heidi shook her head.

"She just said that when she was four, her head got sick and her eyes stopped working."

Jake frowned slightly "Her head?"

Heidi yawned again, and Jake turned off the ignition switch.

"Her brain or something else in her head?"

Heidi was out of the car and halfway up the steps without an answer, and Jake sat still in the silence of the front of his car. *She's blind,* he thought, mystified. He'd never known anyone before who . . . no, that wasn't true. He had met blind people before. Met, kept a polite distance from, and respected from afar.

But Cassie? Jake was still thinking about all the misinterpretations of her he had made, his conscious thought fighting back the realization that it was selfish and cruel but the first thing about her he had understood since meeting her. She had no idea what he looked like. She was not swept away like the other women because the sheer power of his rugged good looks was lost on her.

Jake smiled broadly, feeling the sense of relief finally allowed a foothold. She wasn't oblivious to his attraction, she just couldn't see it. He laughed now, at her, at himself for being worried.

Jake reached for the car door as a second thought struck him just as powerfully as the relief. She didn't like him, and without seeing his good looks and raw physical presence, she never would. Jake tossed the errant thought away and climbed out of the car. *Who cares?* he thought indignantly. There were plenty of women who would be more than happy to see him for who he was.

Maybe I just see through the masks people use to hide who they really are.

Her words to him that night in Mcgoo's rang in his mind as

he walked to the stables slowly. "Maybe if you were the man you are trying to convince everyone you are, I wouldn't have to see anything at all." Jake felt the sting of those words as if she were slapping him with them right now, the jagged tips of every one like a flogging in his heart. What did she see? Who showed up in her mind when she heard his voice, but couldn't see his face? Jake thought back over his words, his abruptness with her, his comments about Natalie, and the way she had become more and more mistrustful in his arms as they danced.

She was misunderstanding; she could only hear and get the wrong impression. That guy who showed up at Mcgoo's was empty and sweet, charming and stealthy. *Casanova.* The actor. Cassie knew Jake Caswell the Hollywood heartthrob, but she had never seen him. Jake stopped suddenly in the dimming light of the sunset.

They all knew Jake Caswell the actor. That was why the women cared nothing about anything but the way he looked. He didn't have to show anyone else more than that, and he didn't want to. Had she been right about him? Had she seen the man he was showing her, and without his looks that guy was a snake? Jake leaned against the doorway to the stables feeling tightness in his chest that made it difficult to breathe. Was that who he had become? Casanova?

*

Jake lost himself in the farm, the mustangs, and the women. Sustaining this complex juggling act kept his mind from sinking into deeper thought. In the weeks since Heidi's revelation about Cassie, Jake found it took more energy than he had to avoid thinking about her and observing her every move. He noticed now the way she held out her hand to meet obstacles, the lift of her nose into the air when a slight breeze would blow, the tilt of her head toward a sound too quiet for most ears. The slight signs that gave away her disability had seemed quirky habits before. They were survival skills, he saw that now. And he wondered how he had ever missed them.

July was excruciatingly hot in the desert. The hard work and the distractions were loosening their grip on his mind, and a part of him thought he should go face Cassie again, but his pride over her rejection, and his stupidity about her blindness kept him trapped on the farm.

His father was growing annoyed with his restlessness and put him to work with the horses for distraction. The sleek black Arabian, Starlight, had been given to Caswell Farms when Miriam had gleaned her herd three years ago. The horse was a beauty, but her canter was far too spirited for therapeutic purposes, and The Rocking J had not had the resources to keep her. Now his father's roan stallion, Ruiando, had taken possession of her, and Jake was going to need to move him and the other mares into the outer corrals before Starlight laid down to birth their colt. He admired her power and beauty and wondered what would be the result of foaling her with Deseo. The prospect of her spirit and Deseo's sheer power intrigued him.

Jake's lack of focus with the cattle was costing him, though. His father had hired Carter part-time, and Jake found himself in infuriating confrontations with the guy daily. As the wave of angry heat rolled from the barn that day, Jake was finished. Finished placating Carter's mean streak, and finished trying to understand the guy's attitude.

"You take the roan out to the paddock." Carter snarled, his hands in fists and a sneer disfiguring his face. "I'll stay with Starlight."

"I don't have time to argue with you about this. Just take the horses out."

"I don't take orders from you, Casanova, and I'll do what I want . . . or whoever I want to. I'm surprised your little friend didn't tell you that."

Jake removed the halters and bridles from the wall and brought them back to Carter. "I have no idea what your problem is, or what you're talking about. Take the horses; the filly is fragile, and I'm staying with her."

Carter threw the bundle of gear to the dirt floor, kicking them back at Jake. "I'm good with fillies. Especially the sleek, high-spirited ones. No one knows how to teach them how to be rode better than me."

Jake shook his head again, in an attempt to ignore Carter's snide remarks. The hint of sinister in the other guy's words suddenly pricked in the back of Jake's heart, and his blood began to race. "Carter, if you think this is going to work, you're dead wrong. Whoever you're threatening or have threatened doesn't change anything. Do your job or get the hell off my property."

"Is that what Lilly was, your property? I was all over her, and there wasn't a damn thing you could do about it."

Jake was turning back to Starlight's stall when the icy fingers of Carter's words seeped into his heart. He whirled back toward Carter.

"Jake!" Robert Caswell's voice was quiet and dark, and Jake automatically took a half step back from Carter's enraged features. Jake's hands uncurled from fists, and he relaxed his furious scowl. Carter's expression only darkened with Robert's appearance but he, too, stepped back from the boiling confrontation. Robert stalked through the swishing of mares' tails to stand between the two young men. Robert's black hair salted with sun and age caught dim lights from inside the horses' stalls.

"I thought the two of you were moving the horses to the pasture. What's the hold up?"

Robert did not dignify the hands with responses when their anger erupted in more shouting. He simply reaffirmed his instructions to them and turned his back to leave as soon as they had both responded with "Yessir."

Heat and tension still hung heavy in the air, but Robert only glared at both of them, then left them to their jobs. Jake strode to the rear of the stable and began haltering the few sorrels that had not made the grazing pasture. Fighting with Carter was a losing proposition, but his dad was right. Carter's problems would have to wait for Starlight's needs to be met first. Carter was silently compliant as well, forking dry straw into Starlight's stable while Jake released the horses into the pasture, turning back to choke on the brown cloud of dust Carter's fancy Ford truck was leaving as he exited Caswell Farms.

Jake coiled the bridles around his fist as he cleared the heavy dirt from his nostrils and glared after the hand. They would have been all right to finish this job if Carter had not started in about Lilly. Jake couldn't afford to let his temper get the best of him, and he was fairly certain that had been exactly what Carter had wanted. Jake spit into the dirt at his feet and fought the urge to call Lilly as fast as he could. Starlight and her foal would not wait for that, and he needed to keep his head.

Glancing at the mares Jake turned back for the horse stable, catching the sound of Ruiando's irritated snorts and clomping feet. Jake picked his pace up to a jog as the horse's discontent grew more desperate, and Jake feared Starlight was in labor.

Chapter Ten

Jake? Cassie thought forlornly, as she twisted her hair into a clump at the back of her head. She was sure to run into him today, and the idea prickled the skin at the back of her neck. He was never close enough for them to have more misunderstandings, but she could feel his eyes on her and his unmistakable presence, almost lurking.

Troy climbed into the truck beside her. "Trailers ready. You?"

"Explain this to me again," she said, latching her seat belt as Troy pulled away from The Rocking J. "Miriam just told me that Heidi won't come to work with Applesauce without Jake, and he's working with the horses today and can't bring her."

As the truck pulled onto the paved highway three miles from Caswell Farms, Cassie rolled down her window and let the warm wind blow across her hot skin.

"So we're taking Applesauce to the farm?" she shouted above the noise.

Troy grunted in affirmation, and Cassie frowned out the windshield. Jake's reckless comments at their last meeting had been more detrimental to Heidi's state of mind than Cassie had realized. Miriam said Debra Caswell was having difficulty getting her anywhere near any of the horses; instead, she shadowed Jake everywhere he went. When Miriam talked to Heidi on the phone, she said she would work with Cassie and Applesauce, but only if she could be where Jake was. Cassie sighed and fought back the trepidation she could feel rolling in her stomach. It was hard enough to work in unfamiliar circumstances, but with Jake hovering nearby . . . she didn't see this going well.

Cassie heard Troy slow down and flip on his blinker. Her body jiggled with the bumps of the truck as the pavement beneath the tires gave way to gravel.

Cassie rolled down her window as they pulled up the gravel driveway, sniffing the air and sorting the smells of cattle, dirt, water, and alfalfa. Turning in her seat, she unfastened her seatbelt, and leaned her head out the window to feel the morning sun from across the cab of the truck. Troy slowed their progress even further as a bawling calf startled Cassie back into the cab.

"Tell me about this place, will you?" she asked, gesturing with her hand out the window, as they started moving again.

"This road goes for about five miles into the heart of the farm. There are a few side roads leading to different pastures and feed buildings. All of the fields between where we turned in and the farm house are alfalfa and corn to the west. And the same except for soy beans on the east."

Cassie frowned as she picked up the slight scent of summer corn but couldn't decipher the soy. "Why do they grow corn and soy?"

A smoky smell drifted on the breeze and she wrinkled her nose.

"They use the corn for feed, and they sell the soy for grain. They grow both because the ground gets depleted of its nutrients when you don't alternate your crop base. Robert and Jake spent a good deal of money and time setting up a fancy irrigation system and reservoir from the San Madera to keep the farm self-sufficient. This part of the country is too hot and dry for the crops that Caswell Farms grows. Thanks to the reservoir and the irrigation, they are the only ones who can do it."

Troy's voice paused, and Cassie rolled her window up to block out the flying dust and acrid smell of smoke now growing stronger. "How did Robert Caswell get permission to take water from the San Madera?"

The uneven travel of the truck paused as Cassie heard the rumble of another vehicle passing by. The pungent odor of the complaining cows overwhelmed all other scents and she listened to Troy once more. "Jake has a government land grant in the San Madera Valley. He found a herd of wild mustangs living near the river and got the grant to protect their native land. Because Caswell Farms uses the irrigation to enrich the land and provide for the natural habitat of the mustangs, there is no mortgage on the farm, and they receive federal funding for its upkeep. That's why Jake spends so much time here, not for the cattle, but for the mustangs. He wants to be involved in their protection."

Cassie nodded, but kept her expression blank as the truck continued to make its way through the alfalfa fields. Jake loved horses? Wild horses? And he was willing to give up screaming fans and fainting women to be near them and care for them? His deep protective instincts of Heidi and Kirstie now seemed to ring a bit more genuinely in her ears, and she frowned as she actually found this part of him somewhat . . . attractive? She shook her head now.

"Sorry," Troy mumbled quietly. "None of that is going to help you find your way around, is it?" Cassie gave a weak smile, and Troy cleared his throat. "When we pull up to the house there will be a six-foot-wide wooden porch with a set of steps that lead to the front door. There is a stone path that leads to them, and I'll drop you off there while I go unload Applesauce in the horse barn. It's about a hundred yards south and west of the house, and the stables are about fifteen feet west of the barn. The stables are a stone structure on the north and wooden on the south. The only access is from the south, and I believe that is where Jake will be birthing a foal. If Heidi is not at the house, you will probably find her down in the stables with him."

Cassie nodded again and unrolled her window as she felt the truck slow.

A gasp escaped Troy's lips, and then the bark of a sharp command as Cassie's nose suddenly filled with caustic smoke and her ears rang with the sound of screaming horses.

"Stay in the truck," Troy snapped as her hand reached for the door handle. She grasped the arm rest tightly as the truck lurched forward and began speeding west away from where they had slowed to stop.

"What's burning?" Cassie yelled as the truck and trailer moved toward the smell and a flare of heat washed back into the truck.

"The stables!" he shouted and then leapt from the driver's side door.

Cassie could hear panicked horses and men rushing about. The heat whipped back across the windshield and smoke grew thick all around her. Despite Troy's instructions, Cassie jumped from the truck and used her cane to make her way to the rear of the truck until she found the trailer. Applesauce's own frightened whinnies met her ears, and she moved around to the side and rear of the trailer until she located the bolt to release the gate.

Letting Applesauce hear her voice, Cassie moved into the trailer and worked her way to the horses twitching head. Taking a lead rope from the rear of the trailer, she hooked it to the horse's bridle and backed her out of the trailer. Cassie could hear the agitation of other animals grouped further down the fence line. The level of anxiety she could feel from them was significantly less, so she told Applesauce to move toward them.

The old gray mare moved faster than Cassie had known she could, stopping at a fence rail and neighing to a few other mares. Cassie tied the lead rope to the fence, patting Applesauce reassuringly and whispering in her ear. Cassie remained with the pastured horses listening and praying that the running men had gotten all of the animals out of the structure.

Troy had said the stable was stone in front, a condition that would reduce the fire's effect, but the wooden portions along with the hay and feed would make it a tinder box, and if there were any horses inside or . . . Jake . . . and maybe Heidi . . . the bitter taste of bile rose into her throat and she fought back smoky tears.

Panic and fear burned up her throat more intensely than that she felt from the fire. Helplessness boiled all around her now, leaving her trapped in its hold. Her hand wrapped around the top rail of the fence where she stood and the world balanced. *Stables to the left,* she thought. *Fence heads north beside the corral.*

Using her cane to feel her way along the fence, Cassie drew closer to the heat and fumes and heard Troy's voice drifting in the wind.

"He's in the northwest corner with Starlight and the foal, but they can't get past the flames. He said if we douse the ceiling on the western side it would help but . . ."

Troy's words were lost as he moved beyond her range and Cassie's heart jumped again. He . . . Jake? Cassie moved further up the fence line, trying to picture in her mind the description of the building Troy had given her. He said it was stone in the front and wood in the rear. It was possible the stone was just a façade, and if she could find a crack or break in it, it would at least give Jake more air.

Cassie stepped away from the fence rail stretching out her arms until her fingertips touched the rail lightly and her other hand was straight out from her side. With the morning sun against her cheek, she stepped away from the rail and toward the scent and heat of the fire. She had taken less than ten steps when her outstretched hand found the outer corrals Troy had told her ran the length of the western wall of the stable. Cassie dropped her cane and climbed under the rails of the corral and worked her way north until she felt the stones of the corner pieces beneath her fingertips.

Collapsing to her knees and trying to ignore the heat and smoke she could feel choking her eyes and throat, Cassie began digging along the cracks of mortar between the smooth stones. Her sensitive fingertips felt for a hint of air seeping from between the edges of the sturdy stone, and her frustration nearly overtook her as there was nothing. Laying her palms against the warm stones, Cassie reached higher until her palm found a stone, scalding beneath her touch, and she pulled back in surprise and elation. The rest had been warm, but the fire's heat had penetrated to engulf this one.

Cassie reached for it again, ignoring all other sensation, to focus on the heat. Running her fingers carefully along its outer edge, she found the mortar dry like clay fired in a kiln.

Cassie dropped back to her knees, pulling a splinter of wood from the corral rail beside her. The wood was dry and brittle in the fire's heat, and the sharp chunk broke away easily.

Cassie found the heated stone again, and then slipped the broken protrusion into the fragile mortar until she felt the hardened grout come away from the rock. Prying beneath it with her fingers and the stick, Cassie managed to dislodge the stone from its placement. She let it fall to the ground at her feet, dropped the awkward pieces of wood, and retrieved the stone. With the heftier weight in her hands, Cassie began battering against the inner wall of the stable.

The space where the rock began breaking through, gushed smoke, pungent with an acidic burnt hide smell mingled with obnoxious chemical fumes.

Cassie instinctually held her breath against the toxins and felt around for the size of the hole in the wall where the stone had been. Smoke poured through the gap, seeking escape, and Cassie became overwhelmed by the choking smell. Coughing uncontrollably for a minute, and gasping on the ground for clearer air, Cassie's eyes watered and stung with the thick air all around her. Tearing a strip from the bottom of her T-shirt, she fell to her knees and reclaimed the fallen rock. She tied the strip of cloth around her mouth and nose, then gripped the rock in both hands.

The shouting of men, crying horses, and even the intermittent shrieks of women's voices drifted only briefly to her ears as Cassie blocked out the swirling sounds and focused only on the sound of rock battering against stone and wood. The roar of the flames reverberated in tempo with the pounding of her arms against the edge of the two-foot gap she had opened up low on the western wall of the stable. As she drew her aching arms back for one more thrust against the building, Cassie caught a low, gasping voice as it drifted through the opening.

"Move back. Get back!"

Cassie scrambled backward until her back collided with a wooden rail in the corral, and she collapsed in a gasp of clear air, sinking back against its support. As she pulled the soot-laden cloth from over her face, she heard once again the sounds of pounding hooves and shouting men, but also the pounding from the inside of the building just feet from her collapse.

The hard crunch of boots on gravel met her ears, as someone rounded the edge of the building to gasp at the scene before him. Cassie guessed from the sharp sound of his exclamation that it was Troy. She grimaced at the sound, figuring Troy had assumed she had stayed where he'd left her in the truck. She could only imagine the scene he was finding now, her face smudged and blackened, in a heap against the corral, staring blankly at what sounded like an explosion of wood and rock burning in a violent thrust from a hole in the stable wall.

Cassie heard the smattering of falling debris. The sounds of rocks and wood raining down all around her. She only felt their proximity as the shards grazed the surface of her skin, close enough to strike her face. Cassie forced herself to remain unmoving. She knew it was the fact that she was oblivious to the onslaught that saved her; had she seen the barrage flying toward her, it was likely she would have tried to dodge the storm and been hit.

"Cassie," Troy shouted. "There is a lot of smoke pouring from the wall. Can you get out of there?"

Cassie began to push herself up from the ground when she heard what sounded like a set of spindly legs and hooves, being shoved through the gap.

"Jake! And the colt," Troy gasped, letting go of his grip on Cassie's wavering attempt at retreat. Cassie felt Troy move away, and she sank back to the rail of the corral. She heard the colt scream and jump to its unsure legs, falling onto the dusty ground before stumbling into another heap at her feet. Cassie laid her head back against the rough wooden rail as she felt and heard Jake crawl through the broken wall and collapse, coughing and choking, on the ground as well.

More shuffling feet and shouts followed, and Cassie heard a voice, deeper than Jake's but eerily similar. "Troy, what's going on?"

Cassie's ears rang with Robert Caswell's panicked voice saying, "Troy, we got Starlight out, but the roof's still burning . . ." His voice broke off abruptly, as she heard Jake's father choke on relief. She imagined the look on Robert's face as he saw Jake push himself onto his hands and knees, coughing spastically and gasping for clean air.

He attempted to speak. The raking of his throat only managed another spasm of coughs as she heard him roll onto his back to get farther away from the still burning timbers of the stable.

"Cassie?" Troy choked, crouching beside her seated against the rail. "How did you? How did you . . . ?"

Troy made a sobbing sound as Cassie wiped her eyes and cheeks, probably smearing soot all over. "Are you okay?"

"I'm fine," she said with a cough, "but Jake needs oxygen and some water. Did anyone call an ambulance?"

Troy's answer was drowned in a screech of fire alarms and ambulance sirens, and Cassie rose to her quavering legs. Troy reached out and grabbed her arm as she ducked beneath the rails to let a group of EMTs pass. Troy took her stumbling feet back to the rail fence she had left so brazenly before. She leaned over the top rail breathing in the warm, crisp air and feeling the faint drops of water from the fire engines spray across her bare arms.

"Are you all right here if I go check on Jake?"

"Troy?" she asked hesitantly. "Did everyone make it out?" Troy put one arm around her shoulders and held her firmly for another minute as he assured her.

"It was Jake and the horses, Cass. The fire wasn't enough to really hurt them, but the fertilizer and the hay and the leather created some sort of noxious gas, and Jake was trapped at the back of the stable with the mare and the foal. He got Starlight far enough through the smoke for us to get to her, but after he went back for the foal, he had inhaled too many fumes, and he couldn't get back through. If you hadn't broken away that gap in the stone . . . " Troy stopped as her shoulders began to convulse against him. He held her more tightly as her body began shaking and her legs gave way beneath her weakening knees.

An hour later, Cassie sat wrapped in a rough woolen blanket on the tailgate of the ambulance. She took deep breaths occasionally from an oxygen mask in her hand, but the shaking had stopped and now she listened only for the words to confirm that Jake was all right.

Debra Caswell sat beside her briefly, making sure she was all right before going to her son's side. Jake had singed his esophagus, and the level of smoke inhalation had lowered his oxidation to frightening levels. He had refused transport, stubbornly insisting he would be fine, but accepting oxygen to help him recover. A few low voices talked quietly around her, but it was the croaking rasp of Jake's voice that brought her face up to find the sound beside her.

"You risked a lot and worked awfully hard to save a guy you don't see much in," he said as he lowered himself onto the tail gate beside her.

Cassie grimaced tightly and then bumped her shoulder against him, "I was actually worried about the horses," she teased with a broken smile. "You were just extra credit."

Jake laughed darkly and then coughed, breaking apart a rattle she heard from his chest. "The horses . . . owe you their lives. But I guess I can relax that I'm free of that debt."

Cassie took a long draw of air from the mask in her palm and smiled weakly, "You don't owe me anything, Jake. I just thought of a way to help, and it was worth a shot."

Jake drew a long breath through his mask as well, then shoved it backwards into the emergency rig.

"That actually makes it so I owe you more. You did all that without seeing anything. In the stable today with the smoke and the smell, I felt as if I were floating in darkness and was paralyzed to know what to do. Troy said you were perfectly safe in the truck and you left it, alone, blind . . . to help with a fire you couldn't see. And, more amazing, you are the one who figured how to get us out."

Cassie tried not to smile at him, but she felt his discomfort as he too noticed that he was rambling.

"I have to admit when I found out you were blind, I felt better about the fact that you don't seem to like me much . . ." he broke off again, and Cassie bit her lip. She was starting to feel a twinge of guilt as he spoke. She had forgotten about their earlier difficulties and hearing the vulnerability in his voice brought it all to the forefront of her thoughts.

"I'm not used to being the victim instead of the hero. How do I reward you for this?"

Jake's hand was suddenly holding her knee, and Cassie's whole body stiffened beneath the familiar tender touch. She heard the edge of charm, dripping from his tongue again.

"It's fine, Jake. You don't owe me anything. I was never in danger, and I would have done what I could no matter who was inside that fire." Cassie stood from her seat and put the mask next to him in the ambulance before she made her away back to Troy's truck.

Climbing in the cab, she slammed the door and stared into familiar nothingness. She was letting him get to her. She couldn't let that happen. The last time she had believed the too-smooth words and tender touches of one of these guys . . . Cassie shook her head, discarding her train of thought as Troy opened the driver's side door beside her.

"You ready to go home, super girl?" he teased, climbing up into the truck. Cassie cast her eyes toward his voice and grimaced.

"Do me a favor, would you? Let's keep my part in this little disaster a secret. The last thing I want is for Miriam to worry about me every time I'm away from The Rocking J."

"Too late," he stated cheerily. "Debra has already been on the phone with Miriam, she knows the whole story."

Troy laughed and then cleared his throat to stifle it as he maneuvered the truck back onto the dirt road leading away from Caswell Farms. Cassie sat silently on the drive towards the highway and throughout the quiet trip back.

*

When they arrived at The Rocking J, Miriam met them with concern and congratulations. Everyone had a thousand questions about what happened, but Cassie remained quiet and serious amid the barrage. Troy filled Miriam in on details, and Cassie tried to withdraw from the attention.

After Miriam hugged her and she found her way back to her apartment above the garage, Cassie took a long hot shower and took the rest of the day off. She attempted listening to one of her audio books, as well as catching up on her therapy notes, but every time her mind was too still, the sound of Jake's apology drifted through her thoughts. No matter how hard she tried, she couldn't untangle the sweet charming hiss of her past snake winding with Jake's rasping cough.

"Cassie!" Jana's voice along with the pounding of her fists against the door woke Cassie from her unintended nap on her futon. Her book sounded softly in her ears as she shut the digital player off and rubbed her bleary eyes. Pressing her palms against her eye sockets, Cassie attempted to hold back the headache now trying to claw its way free of her pounding skull.

Jana battered the door again, and Cassie stood, walking to the door and unlocking the deadbolt. Before she could open it all the way, Jana pushed inside, dragging Cassie with her to collapse on the narrow love seat.

"Cassie," Jana said. "I just heard about the fire. Are you all right? Is Jake? What happened? How did you get to him?"

Jana's questions were flung like machinegun fire, and Cassie waited for a break in her assault before answering.

"I'm fine, Jana. Jake is all right too, I hope," she added suddenly concerned that maybe she had left too quickly to really know the answer to that question. She shook her head briefly and focused her wandering thoughts back on Jana's frantic questions. "I don't know how the fire started or how I found him. I just wanted to help get some air to him . . . them."

Jana's voice became an interrogation. "Them? Did Jake have someone with him, and that's why you look so irritated when you say he's fine?"

Cassie pulled back sharply from Jana and glared with her mouth pinched. "Them," she enunciated, "is him and the foal. He was in the rear with a brand-new colt and neither of them could get out."

Jana sighed with heavy relief in the sound. "Good, you only get that look on your face when he's done something charming for some girl. If I didn't know you better I would think you were jealous."

Cassie's mouth dropped open with Jana's teasing and her mind wanted to argue the point, but Jana was right. *He bothers me too much,* she thought guiltily.

Cassie wrinkled her brow and bit her lip. "No wonder he keeps trying with me. If I'm acting as if I'm jealous, he would think I'm interested."

"I would think he's used to random girls being jealous of his attentions on other women. It probably bothers him that he's being punished for another man's mistakes."

Cassie rose from the love seat and went to her small kitchen.

Retrieving two bottles of water, she gave one to Jana and took the lid off her own. Her thoughts fought against Jana's words as she felt her iron grip squeeze the liquid onto her hand.

"What? What do you mean?"

Jana took a long sip from her bottle and waited as Cassie dried her hand and carpet with a dishtowel before carefully answering. "I don't think Jake is your problem. I think you're trying to punish him because what you'd like to do is pummel Dylan."

Cassie stopped rubbing the carpet in front of her and fought back the sting of tears. After that first night with Jana at Mcgoo's, she told Jana about Dylan Haskins, her ex-fiancé. Now the sound of his name in this conversation suddenly called forth angry tears, and she knew Jana was right. Regardless, just because Dylan was a snake with blue eyes, she did gain one good thing from her experience with him; she developed the ability to hear lies disguised as truth in the tone and tenor of a man's voice.

"You never met Dylan, Jana," Cassie said tartly. "If you could hear the similarities, you would recognize the need for me to at least be irritated with Jake."

Cassie took the damp towel back to the kitchen as she let Jana muse silently over her words. When she came back into the room and sat beside Jana again, Cassie felt the awkward tension of unfinished conversation between them. There was no way to explain this to a sighted person, and there was no way for her to see what Jana was trying to point out to her. After another moment of silence, Jana sighed.

"Miriam wanted me to tell you she's doing Dutch oven tonight just for you, so make sure you come down for dinner, okay?"

Cassie smiled mirthlessly and took another drink from her bottle. "I'm sorry, Jana," she said as her friend stood to leave. "These scars are old and deep, and I really don't want to work on getting over it with some part-time cowboy. If you are right about this, then Jake's better off, too."

Jana squeezed Cassie's hand before opening her door and stepping out onto the narrow staircase. "Jake has scars, too, Cassie. Why do you think he never stays focused on one girl for too long?"

The sound of the wooden door slipping into its casing seemed to reverberate in Cassie's head. Of course Jake had scars; he wasn't hiding them that well. Who was he beneath those scars, and could she take a chance that it was even worth looking?

Chapter Eleven

"Jake?" His mother's voice drifted beneath his bedroom door.

Jake immediately turned his face into his thick cotton pillow to muffle another coughing spell, to keep his mother's worried face from appearing in his room again. His chest and throat burned with the remnants of the fire, and he stayed in bed, lacking the energy to do anything else. His mind flashed back to when his survival instincts had dissipated with the lack of oxygen in his blood, and he'd heard the constant pounding of Cassie's rock against the stable wall.

Crouched on the floor near the wall at the back of the stable, Jake had pressed his face as near to the floor as he could. In the blinding smoke and fumes, his fingers located a splintered board, allowing a whisper of air, where Ruiando had kicked them loose.

In the smoky darkness, Jake heard only the sounds of help just beyond his sight. When the stone had fallen away and air poured into his suffocating vacuum, his mind had cleared and instinct and anger took over.

Freedom from that prison had only brought on new shackles, though. The prospect of death had seemed impossible-until he had realized that living burned, scarred, and mutilated by flame would have been worse. When he had washed away the soot from the fire, he noticed a deep chemical burn that was sensitive to the touch beneath his tan, and in his mind his features had melted like molten wax. Every time he looked in the mirror, he could only see the dissolution of everything he was . . . and wasn't.

He shook his head, then dressed and went down to breakfast.

*

"Jake," his mother snapped before he'd barely had a chance to sit. "It's been two weeks. You have to do something besides go to the reservoir and work on the irrigation." Jake looked up from his breakfast to see his mother's bright blue eyes flinging daggers at him like a Chinese knife thrower. Jake pushed away from the table where he had been picking at his food. Glancing at Heidi's oblivious expression across from his seat, Jake stood and took his nearly full plate to the sink before turning back to face his fuming mother.

"What are you suggesting I do? Dad's been crazed with the beef buyers and rebuilding the stables. Someone has to take care of the reservoir and the other chores. If I'm not helping out enough, tell me what I haven't gotten to yet and I'll do it first, but I have work to do on Mustang Mountain."

Debra rolled her eyes at his sullen speech, and she grinned wickedly in response.

"Oh, I want you on the mountain. I just don't want you up there from sunrise to sunset . . . alone." Jake opened his mouth to argue with her as he stepped away from the sink, but his mother held up her hand, and he pinched his mouth again. "I know you have a lot to do up there, baby," she crooned, moving to stand in front of him and running the palms of her hands over his twitching arms. "I just think you shouldn't be so isolated."

Jake groaned inwardly. Isolation was exactly what he wanted; no one looking at him, no idle hands or thoughts to prick at the hollow in his heart that the fire had left behind. No questions to answer about who he was and where he belonged . . . *or with whom,* he thought bitterly. His phone and messages had been full and unopened for over a week now, and he didn't want to talk about any of it. The reservoir was perfect escape and excuse for hiding his restlessness.

"It will be after three when they get there, and they have to go before sunset so it won't be that long. Just help out Miriam since

Troy is down with the flu, and I'll leave you to your moping for another couple of weeks."

Debra's voice was pleading and Jake's distracted thoughts scrambled to keep up with her speech.

"What?" he asked, uncrossing his arms and stepping back from her. "Who is coming after three? Coming where?"

His mother frowned, and Jake thought he could see her mentally making an appointment with a therapist for him. His thoughts drifted more and more lately, and just yesterday she asked him if he needed to be signed up for sessions at The Rocking J along with Heidi.

"Miriam wants to take her muscular dystrophy kids swimming, and I volunteered the San Madera Reservoir. I just need you to spend a few hours helping . . . and maybe flirting with her counselors . . . today."

Jake scowled openly now and started to push past her. Reaching out and grabbing him around his broad shoulders, Debra begged him with her eyes.

"Please, Jake, if you're there, Heidi will go, too. I don't know how to get her to go back to working with Cassie."

Jake rolled his eyes and glanced at his sister's long hair swaying as she sang along with her MP3 player at the kitchen table.

"What are you talking about, Mom? For the past few weeks she's bugged me every day to go see Cassie so she can make sure she's okay."

Debra glanced backward at Heidi, then turned back to Jake, dropping her voice. "She has been to check on Cassie, but every time Cassie wants to get on the horses with her, Heidi wants to go find you. I'm lucky I got her to agree to go swimming. When she found out Cassie was going, she said she would only go if you went, too. Please, honey," Debra said again. "It's just a couple of hours."

Jake growled low in his chest and fought off the urge to cough with the sound. Maybe Cassie would be a buffer between him and Miriam's girls if she had to work with him.

As much as he had been avoiding the world, Cassie had been his exception. She was safe, she didn't care, and she wasn't any more interested in impressing him than he was with impressing anyone else right now. Miriam had taken Ruiando, Starlight, and the colt, Firestorm, onto the ranch after the stables had been demolished. The only human interaction Jake had allowed himself since then had been checks of the horses with Cassie. She had not pushed him for more, and he had not tried. Their quiet ability to be together but separate was something he found comforting. It was this companionship that teetered the scales for him now.

"Fine, Mom. Three o'clock."

*

Jake watched from the edge of the dock as the van and truck from The Rocking J pulled up to the ramp leading onto the wooden surface that would allow the wheelchairs access to the San Madera Reservoir. The van's sliding door opened, and Miriam jumped from the driver's seat as Jake approached. With her back to him, she began chattering excitedly about the reservoir and her thanks to him for being there. She had managed to lower two of the chairs on the lift and was strapping a third to the base when Jake began moving a pair of blond girls away from the lowering lift, smiling and winking at the blushing girls. With their shrunken musculature and weakened frames, it was difficult to assess their age, but Jake figured they were mostly between six and twelve years old. The smallest was a dark-haired boy with an angry scowl etched into his deep set eyes and sunken cheeks.

"We are all going to drown," he complained in a high plaintive voice. "This is nuts."

Jake smiled conspiratorially at the boy, then pointed toward a small narrow fiberglass boat dockside. "If you put one of those life jackets on," he promised, gesturing towards the pile in Jana's arms, "you and I will go out in the skiff and run lifeguard patrol. Then you will be safe in your jacket, and I can keep anyone who is crazy enough to brave the water from drowning. Deal?"

The fear and doubt in the boy's eyes suddenly fled with Jake's offer, and Miriam nodded approval as she finished unloading those willing to swim.

Jana began strapping life preservers on the small-framed kids, and Jake squatted on his heels to do the same for his new first mate.

"I'm Jake," he said, grinning at the gap-toothed boy. "What's your name?"

Jake kept his eyes on the boy as he lifted him out of the awkward machinery and began carrying him to the water craft.

"Kyle," the boy squeaked anxiously as they drew nearer to the boat.

Jake walked into the shallow water by way of the rocky beach until he stood thigh deep in the cold mountain run off. He lowered Kyle into a seat strapped to the stern. Jake buckled him to the back rest and kept one hand on the boy's shoulder. Jake pointed to the line tethering the boat to the dock and smiled warmly at Kyle again. "That rope will keep you right here while I go help with the others. Can you keep your eyes on it until I get back, and shout my name if you need me?" Kyle nodded with a bite of his bottom lip, and Jake slowly backed out of the water.

Keeping one eye focused on Kyle, Jake helped Miriam and Jana ready the other kids and lower them into the group flotation device.

"Where's Cassie?" Jake asked looking around. "Where's Heidi?"

Miriam smiled as she sat on the dock next to where Kyle bobbed in the boat.

"They are both still in the truck with Chris. Cassie convinced Heidi to bring Applesauce and Jackpot up for a trail walk, but now Heidi is refusing to get out of the truck."

Jake frowned darkly and looked back at the windshield silver in the afternoon light. "Should I go try to help?" he asked as the repetitive sound of Cassie's cane tapped onto the dock behind him.

Jake turned toward the approach of Cassie's auburn hair, burnt orange in the light. "Is Heidi all right?" he asked, moving toward her and reaching out his hands to stop her march toward him. As Cassie struck Jake's outstretched palms she paused, planting her feet and then stepping back from him.

"Jake, when you are finished with the kids could you come help me with Heidi?" The frustration in her voice rubbed at Jake's nerves.

"If you're not in the mood for her today . . ." Jake said cautiously, crossing his arms in front of him.

Cassie's expression flashed shock for a moment, and then she frowned. "It's not her, Jake. I just don't like feeling that her progress is reliant on anyone else. I feel as if I'm encouraging codependence in her by even agreeing to ask, but I think we can get her on Applesauce today if she knows you are close by. I may be able to teach her to trust the horse and relinquish her grip on you."

Jake nodded and looked into the silver surface of the truck's windshield. Jake narrowed his eyes suspiciously at the truck, and he turned slowly back to face Cassie.

"Tell her that I have made a promise to a six-year-old boy, and I expect her to work with you while I keep it." Cassie broke into a wide smile as she turned away from him. He continued, "Tell her I expect her to trust me, and that means she is going to do this without me."

Jake shook his head as Cassie disappeared behind the horse trailer. He knew Heidi was just punishing him for teasing her about leaving for Wyoming. *This is ridiculous,* Jake mentally complained as he pulled his T-shirt over his head and jumped into the cold water beside the boat.

The warm air and chilled water sent a shiver across his back. As he turned and climbed into the boat behind Kyle, he caught Jana's wide-eyed stare. With the quiver of his flesh and a brief rekindling of his old confidence burning across his cheeks, he smiled into her dark brown eyes. She dropped her eyes into the rubber float, and

Jake felt satisfaction. Women looked at him like that all the time; he hungered for that expression to cross a woman's face, it meant he had her.

The sound of Cassie and Heidi emerging with the horses from the trailer reminded him that Cassie had looked at him that way, too, when he had talked of his promise to Kyle. He had never seen that look on her face before, and she had discarded it as quickly as it had appeared.

Jake consciously took stock of it as he started the motor and steered the boat out beyond the buoy, far enough away to keep Kyle entertained and near enough to jump to the rescue if necessary. Jake pointed out to Kyle the bubbles coming to the surface as the trout saw the flash of sunlight dappling the water and rose to nibble at its color above them.

The afternoon sun shone on the placid water like lemon-drop diamonds against the deep blue of the mountain lake. The chatter of birds and excitement of screaming children broke the warm sky for the next two hours. Jake spent the time keeping an eye out for Miriam and Jana, but the majority of his long hours were spent focused on Kyle.

He motored the small boat slowly around the reservoir, pointing out the lava dam and spillway, the intricate tangle of pipes and spigots protruding for the irrigation system, the rushing inlet of higher creeks and the marshy stretch of forest east of where the bold San Madera thundered through the canyon.

While he and Kyle were catching frogs along a sand bar, Jake noticed Cassie and Heidi seated in a deep green meadow beyond the gray edge of the access road. Applesauce and Cassie's Jackpot were bridled and saddled, but Jake could tell from Heidi's pinched features that she wasn't happy about it. Sighing in disappointment, Jake took an empty bait can from the bottom of the boat and placed Kyle's newest bullfrog into the bottom. Scooping in a handful of water and handing it back to the bright-eyed boy, Jake turned his attention back to the shrieks of laughter from the flotation.

Taking the frog and the boy back to the buoy, Jake settled back into the boat to watch the swimmers and chase the icy chill from his shoulders, where he had immersed them in the water for frog duty. He was tempted to lay his head back and close his eyes, but the boat rocked beneath the excited little boy's feet as he played with the irritated swamp frog, and the splashing of his charges kept his mind too alert to relax into the summer heat.

Heidi appeared at the edge of the dock before Jake had registered her movement, diving into the cold water and swimming to Miriam and Jana. Her formerly pinched features were smooth now and light as she splashed and dove beneath the float, tickling the feet of the children. When Jake looked back up again, the horses were tied to the fence beside the truck where Chris Barben fed and unsaddled them, and Cassie was making her way with her red-tipped cane down the dock. Kyle handed Jake the bait can, insisting he needed more water for Bullworth, and Jake leaned over the side to scoop some more into the can as he watched Cassie walk closer and closer to where the dock ended and the deep water of the reservoir began.

Panic swelled through Jake as he saw her nearing the drop off. His mind never considered the idea that even if she went over the side, she could probably swim. She was blindly, literally, heading for danger, and Jake was about to jump to his feet to keep her from falling from the dock. Then he remembered he was in the boat with Kyle, too far away to stop her, and he watched helplessly.

Cassie walked slowly but confidently down the wooden planked dock until her cane struck the edge, two steps before she would have stepped off. She dropped the cane beside her and shimmied her jeans over her hips and knees until she stepped out of them. She folded them carefully and set them beside the cane, then pulled her T-shirt over her ginger hair.

Jake clamped his jaw tightly as the sinking sun illuminated

her from behind and her body became silhouetted against the burnished sky.

She was tall for a girl, and her long legs were lean and sculpted into an hourglass at her hips. Her skin was tanned from the summer sun, and her long hair fell over slender shoulders and a graceful neck. She was . . . beautiful. He had always thought she was pretty, but he was surrounded by attractive women, and she had never stood out from the rest before. As he watched her lean lithe form move to the end of the dock and slide smoothly into the water, he really looked. Against her beige skin, her pale blue eyes picked up sparks of blue flame from the water and flashed in the light. She had piled her long reddish-brown waves in a twist at the top of her head; a wisp or two escaped to fall beside her cheeks and jaw as she held onto the float and chatted with Jana and Miriam.

He was mesmerized by the sight. Jake felt himself let go of something as he stared at her face. She was gorgeous, sexy, a vision that would have rivaled some of the women he knew from Hollywood. Why had he never seen it before?

A screech from Kyle brought Jake's mind back to the boat as he realized he'd dropped Kyle's frog habitat into the water.

Kyle's shrieks and the splashing descent of the can brought Jana and Miriam's attention to see what had happened. Jake couldn't get his eyes off of Cassie fast enough, and it seemed as if he couldn't drag them away at all.

"Jake?" Miriam's voice broke his transfixed gaze to follow the can to the blacker depths of the reservoir beneath him and Kyle's perch. "Are you . . . is everybody all right?" she asked choking back a laugh, as Kyle continued to shriek.

"Yeah, yeah," Jake fumbled, trying to quiet Kyle. "I dropped his can. Kyle, relax I've got another one in the bait shed. Just hold the frog, and we'll go back."

Jake started the motor again, and Kyle complained loudly as he moved the small boat back to the side of the dock, keeping his eyes fixed firmly on the bow of the wooden structure. He wouldn't look their way again; he may never be able to look at her again, at least not ever the same.

*

"Jake?" Miriam's voice broke across his concentration as he ate potato salad. Miriam was just finishing up feeding the picnic to her horde and Jake had taken the plate she had fixed for him to the dock. He sat, legs dangling in the water, sun drying his shorts and hair in the dusky light. "Have you seen Cassie or Heidi?"

Jake twisted his upper body around to squint into the blaring sunset behind the vehicles. "Not since dinner," he said, now scanning the water's edge for movement. The aspen groves lay in breezeless silence, and Jake stood, picking up his plate and stalking to the end of the dock. "Are the horses still tied to the fence?" he asked throwing his trash into a barrel at the ramps edge.

"No." Miriam said with a frown. "Cassie told Chris that she was taking Jackpot into the lower meadow to graze, but I thought she would be back by now."

Jake pulled his T-shirt over his head again and bent to put his shoes on. "Did she say if she was going to the meadow she and Heidi were in this afternoon? The wild horses come to the lower meadows in the evenings. Without their winter coats, they prefer the lower lands at night."

Miriam shook her head, looking around. "I've got to get the kids loaded and back to The Rocking J before sunset, so Jana and I are leaving. Chris said he would stay if she and Heidi don't get back in time, but I'm getting worried."

Jake nodded, his eyes still perusing the area for movement. Turning for the road Jake caught sight of the swish of Applesauce's tail in the trailer, and his mind grasped an idea. "I'll take Applesauce," he shouted over his shoulder to Miriam, "I'll see if I can get them back here before you leave."

Miriam smiled warmly at him as he pulled the gray mare from the trailer and bridled the animal.

"I appreciate you letting us come today, Jake. You were great with Kyle, and . . . except for that mishap with the frog can, he is impressed with you, too."

Jake blushed deeply, seeing those few minutes in his mind outlined like Cassie in his memory.

"I . . . he . . ." Jake gulped and coiled the bridle in his hand as he shifted on the gravel. "Tell him I'm sorry about that." He stammered, unsure why a lost bait can seem so important. Miriam smiled again and squeezed his arm tenderly.

"It's fine, Jake, you weren't dangerously distracted, just . . . a man."

Jake's blue eyes flashed briefly as he realized Miriam had clearly seen the reason for his lost focus, and he grimaced guiltily until she laughed at his discomfort.

"Give it a shot, Jake," she said quietly gesturing with her head toward the meadows. "They don't all turn out like Melinda."

Jake tightened his jaw and took a shaky breath, "I'll be right back," he promised, vaulting bareback onto Applesauce and prodding the old horse down the winding dirt road.

*

Jake cursed under his breath. The methodical plod of the tired horse wove memories of Melinda through his head; her dark hair tangling in the wind, riding bareback through knee-high grass, the fullness of her fleshy pink lips. The hollow place inside his heart throbbed as thoughts of Cassie overshadowed memories of Melinda. It was almost painful to see her . . . here. The picture he had carried in his mind for so long was of another dark-haired beauty who would never visit this place, never spend an afternoon in the reservoir, and never ride the high aspens with him ever again.

Coming to the edge of the meadow, he saw the woman whose presence now claimed his thoughts. Jake slid from Applesauce's back and walked toward Cassie. Heidi and Jackpot were with her. The mare was Cassie's specially trained horse. According to some of the girls at The Rocking J, Cassie had worked in Albuquerque with a group of Natchez Indians who had taught her and the horse special signals for communicating.

Heidi was standing in the long, green-yellow grass watching as Jackpot grazed and Cassie showed her how to stroke the neck of the animal, but Heidi would do nothing more than look apprehensively at the horse. As Heidi looked up to see him approach through the meadow, Jackpot's ears twitched and perked. Cassie immediately stood facing the blaze of western sky and listened for some indication of who moved toward them in the grasses.

"It's Jake," he called out knowing both Cassie and Heidi would not be able to tell who was moving toward them in the setting sun.

"Yake," Heidi called out with a frown. "Where have you been?"

Jake stopped short of where they stood, dropping Applesauce's reins into the grass and letting the horse graze contentedly. "I told you, Heidi, I made promises to someone else, and what kind of a big brother would I be if I didn't keep my promises to everyone, not just you?"

Jake smiled as he looked at Cassie, silent beside his sister. Her face remained blank, and the brief smiles he had seen earlier were still holding their position behind her brilliant blue eyes. He felt stupid; what was he thinking, smiling at Cassie? He didn't even want to charm her, not to mention waste a perfect smile on a woman who couldn't even appreciate it.

"Miriam is packing up to go. She has to get the kids back before sunset."

Cassie lifted her chin slightly and focused into the disappearing light. "Wow!" she exclaimed, clicking her tongue against her teeth as Jackpot raised her head and nudged Cassie's shoulder with her nose. "I lost track of time out here. It feels like it's nearly seven." Jake looked over his shoulder at the onyx mountain and the lengthening shadows, turning back to both her and Heidi.

"It's actually only six. The sun sets earlier on the mountain, so it feels later."

A knowing expression crossed Cassie's face, and he could almost see her make mental calculations in her head for the higher hills. Jake reached out to take Heidi by the hand and began pulling her toward Applesauce, hearing Cassie and Jackpot follow closely behind.

"It's a long way, Heidi. And it's steep back to the reservoir. If I ride with you, will you let Applesauce take us back up to the truck?" Jake felt Heidi stiffen and plant her feet beside him, but he continued to hold her hand and walk to take the horses reins, dangling in the grass. "Come on, sweetie. I'll ride with you, all you have to do is sit in front of me and hold on. I'll do the rest."

Heidi's eyes were wide and wild, and she looked back over her shoulder at Cassie. "I . . . no. I . . . can't, Yake."

Cassie reached out and took Heidi's other hand, squeezing it tightly. "He couldn't come help before because he was keeping a promise Heidi. He's making you one now, and you have seen that he keeps his promises."

Heidi nodded, biting her bottom lip and looking up into Jake's eyes. "If I ride with you, Yake," she said hesitantly, "you have to promise me that no matter if you have to go, you will always come back. If I ride this horse, you can't decide that it means you don't have to come home anymore. I can't go to Wyoming, Yake. Even if I could ride."

Jake dropped his sister's hand and turned to face her. Grabbing her shoulder, he shook her a little and looked into her frightened eyes. "Listen, Heidi, I don't come home to help you with Applesauce. I don't come back because I like the mustangs better than you, and I don't come back because I have to, even though

I like Wyoming. I come back because this is home." Tears rolled down Heidi's cheeks now as she leaned against his chest, wetting his shirt with her fears.

"You only came back for Melinda, and then the mustangs. You say lots of things to pretty girls that you don't mean, and you always go Yake, always."

Jake heaved a sigh and put both arms around his little sister. "You're right." He breathed into her hair. "I do say lots of things to pretty girls, and I do have to go sometimes, but, Heidi, I never make them promises I don't keep, and I promise you, I will always come back. Always."

Heidi nodded against him, drying her cheeks and taking deep breaths, "Okay, Yake, I'll ride with you."

Jake mounted the gray mare and pulled Heidi up to sit in front of him as Cassie handed him the reins. He was struck by the soft curve of her mouth as she offered a tender, approving smile. She mounted her horse, and they began plodding out of the meadow. As Applesauce moved beneath him and Heidi, Jake felt the girl stiffen at the swaying motion. He wrapped one arm firmly around her waist, gripped the reins tightly, and told her to hold the horse's mane as well.

Cassie and Jackpot walked quietly beside them, encouraging Heidi to feel the movements of the horse instead of bracing herself against them. As the horses climbed, Heidi relaxed, allowing the trip to proceed without complaint. Quietly they walked onto the road and then north into the tall trees. The horse's hooves were only interrupted by the birds and their own deep breathing as they meandered.

Jake watched Cassie as she rode. Her horse was unsaddled as well, and Jake admired the line of her lean body pressed into the flanks of the horse's flesh. She moved with the animal, occasionally whispering quietly and stroking her mane with deft hands, asking the horse to drop behind or in front of Applesauce. Her eyes glowed with the depth of the apparent trusting relationship she shared with this horse. She pressed her face against Jackpot's neck and smiled fondly.

"How long have you been blind?" Jake suddenly asked as Cassie raised her head from the horse's mane.

"Most of my life, since I was four years old."

"What happened?"

"When I was about two and a half, my parents noticed that I was running into things more and more. My mom would find me with my ears pressed against the door listening to the outside world, but I wouldn't go into it. My dad said I liked the feel of the refrigerator vibrating beneath my palms. Before I would walk to another room, I would find the vibrations in the floorboards until I located a wall. I would follow the surface with my fingers into other rooms. My parents were concerned when I wouldn't look at books, or watch TV, so they took me to an optometrist and then an ophthalmologist, who eventually sent me to an oncologist."

Jackpot snorted and shook his head, just as Jake was going to warn Cassie about a low hanging branch protruding across the road. Instead, Cassie dropped her face back to lean against the mare's neck as the branch passed overhead.

"An oncologist?" Jake asked as she raised her head. "Cancer?"

Cassie nodded her head and then shrugged. "I had tumors growing all along my optic nerves, and they were interfering with the transference of images to my brain. They did everything they could—operations and chemotherapy—but eventually in order to ensure that the cancer didn't spread to my brain, my parents opted to have my optic nerves removed."

Jake couldn't hold back a slight gasp, and Cassie grimaced at the sound. "I don't know if that's exactly what happened, or if that's just how they explained it to me. The point is my eyes work, there's just no connection to my brain."

"They took out your optic nerves? That seems kind of extreme."

Cassie tossed her hair back from her face and shrugged. "Maybe," she said, "but if you came to me and told me the person I loved had a time bomb ticking behind their eyes, I would have no problem trading their sight for their life."

"It wasn't just your sight though, Cassie," he insisted. "Haven't you ever wondered what dreams you might have chased if you could see? You are pretty amazing with these horses and the therapy, but you have to admit, you are never going to be an airline pilot or a race car driver."

Cassie laughed, a sound like bells through the trees surrounding them. "I think I'm all right with that, Jake. I don't think those ever would have been my dreams anyway."

Jake frowned as Heidi elbowed him in the ribs and asked to get off the horse. "I want to walk in front of her," Heidi grumbled. "My butt hurts."

Jake grinned at Heidi, but then pulled Applesauce to a stop and helped Heidi slide awkwardly to the ground. Slipping from the horse's back, Jake could hear the sound of Miriam's voice ahead and Cassie's thighs rubbing against Jackpot's hide as she also dismounted. They walked in the direction of the trailer, close enough for their hands to graze each other's once or twice.

"Aren't you angry, though, someone else stole your dreams and now you have to clean up the aftermath?"

"I've had dreams, Jake, like everyone else. Dreams that are just that . . . dreams. Not all of them can come true."

"That's not fair. Other people make choices and you have to live with a broken dream?"

Cassie sighed and reached out to squeeze his hand beside her own. "No, Jake," she said firmly. "You dream a better dream."

Chapter Twelve

"Jake?" Cassie asked over her shoulder, as she handed the horses off to Troy for stabling. "You want to talk about Jake?"

When Debra Caswell had arrived that afternoon, Heidi was riding bareback on Applesauce. Even though Cassie still needed to accompany her on the horse, Heidi's progress since the ride with Jake was remarkable. Heidi was fascinated with the animal; the unalterable patience of the horse was providing Heidi more confidence every day.

"Jake and I are not that close, Mrs. Caswell. I'm not sure I could tell you anything."

"I am actually interested in your professional opinion, Cassie, and please, call me Debra."

Cassie attempted an untroubled smile, but she could feel that it had come across more anxious than she intended.

"Okay . . . Debra, I'll do my best."

Cassie located her white cane, unfolded it, and began moving along the fence line, unclear as to whether or not Debra was following. Heidi went up ahead, and Cassie heard the sound of her voice mingled with Troy's as Debra and Cassie approached.

"I don't know if you've noticed," Debra began nervously, "but Jake is becoming withdrawn and distant. He is isolating himself from the other parts of his life, and I see something in his eyes I haven't seen for a while."

"Something? What do you see?"

"He's . . . tortured, haunted almost. I hear him at night, trying not to cough, or make a fuss, but I know he's not sleeping. He hasn't been to Mcgoo's or out with any of his friends since the fire, and I think it may have triggered an old memory."

"What kind of memory? You said you saw this . . . something in him a while ago. How long ago?"

Debra stopped, and Cassie felt her hand reach out and slow Cassie's progress too.

"This is not the first fiery tragedy Jake has survived. The other one was much worse, but is it possible he is traumatized just the same as he was then?"

"Without knowing much about Jake's history, I can't really say. Post-traumatic stress occurs after experiences like a fire, to one degree or another, but I don't know about this other one. What happened?"

Debra took a shuddering breath. and Cassie felt the older woman's hand grow cold against her warm skin.

"Jake and some of his friends were in an accident where the truck caught fire."

Cassie nodded, and tried not to picture Jake in that circumstance. It was difficult to keep an objective viewpoint if she saw it in her mind.

"Were they hurt? What happened? Give me an idea of what Jake might be dealing with."

Cassie wrapped her hand around Debra's, which was trembling against her arm. Cassie braced herself for the details as Debra talked, finally understanding why Jake had been so close, yet so distant lately.

"He was in a truck, on his way home from a graduation party with his girlfriend and her brother. They were coming down from Navajo Canyon, and they missed a curve on the narrow canyon road. The truck rolled six times, and Jake was buckled inside when it started burning."

Cassie winced openly, trying not to paint gruesome pictures in her mind of the scene.

"How did they get out? Debra, I know this is bringing up painful memories for you, too, but if the fire retriggered the trauma in Jake, then he may be reliving something else, too. I need to know as much about it as I can so I know how to help him."

"Jake got himself and Carter out by undoing the seatbelts and climbing through the broken windshield, but . . ."

"Carter . . . Carter Langdon?"

"Yes, Carter was Melinda's brother. They were twins."

Cassie gasped. "I heard Jake and Heidi talking about someone named Melinda, but I had no idea." Debra sniffed a little, and Cassie's mind formed another picture with the sound. "They *were* twins? As in past tense?"

"When the truck rolled, Melinda had been sitting on the console between the seats. The windshield shattered in the rollover, and she was thrown out of the truck. It rolled over her as it fell down the side of the canyon road."

Cassie was staring wide eyed at Debra's face, seeing nothing but the horror she could feel hanging between her and Debra.

"Was Jake driving?" Cassie asked quietly. "Does he blame himself for the accident?"

"Jake tried to take the keys away from Carter so he could drive, but Carter was drunk and wouldn't let Jake have them. Jake wasn't even supposed to be in the truck that night. He and Melinda had gone to the party together, but when Carter got drunk and wanted to leave, Melinda wouldn't let him go alone. Jake couldn't talk them into going with him. He went hoping to talk Carter into letting him drive. Does he blame himself for it? Absolutely."

Debra punctuated her last statement, and Cassie blew out a shaky breath.

"He saved her brother from the fire, but he couldn't save her," Cassie stated to clarify.

"Worse than that." Debra sighed. "He walked away without a scratch on him. Carter tore his shoulder up pretty bad, and he was on track to be the next team roping champion at the national finals rodeo. He has never been able to rope since that night, and he blames Jake."

Cassie sighed again, still shaking her head.

"Is that why Jake doesn't drink? I have been with him at Mcgoo's and he always has a drink, but I have never smelled anything but cola on him. I thought that was strange for a guy who picks up women in bars."

Debra didn't respond as Heidi's soft bubbly voice skipped up next to them.

"I'm ready, Mom. I want to go tell Yake about riding today, let's go."

Debra reached out quickly and took Cassie's hands in her own.

"Thank you, Cassie, for all your help and all you will be able to do with . . ."

Cassie tried not to frown at Debra as she thanked her again and left with Heidi. *I do not want to know this much about Jake,* she argued internally. *It makes him too tragic of a hero.*

The smell of dusty earth and horse hair mingled in Cassie's nose as she left the barn's enclosure to begin her notes on Heidi's session. Running her fingers along the smooth painted surface of the barn's door, she turned her face away from the sun and felt the hot afternoon light against her hair. With skilled, practiced hands she began swinging the tip of her cane above the graveled dirt high enough so as not to catch the rutted drive that would be underfoot in the next thirteen steps.

As Cassie's feet took her from the barn to the ranch house, they paused with the slight change in inclination of the road. She focused her attention on the path of her travel. If even a few feet off track, Cassie would miss the end of the wide porch near the kitchen door, and she and the chickens would end up fighting over who was going to escape the coop first. Cassie wrinkled her nose at the smell of feather fumes that wafted toward her. Side stepping away from the sound of the creaking coop, Cassie held her breath. The hens were particularly pungent today, and once again she found her thoughts lost in barring the smell from her senses.

As she turned her nose to breathe air not fowl, she caught a brief scent of soap and skin before colliding headlong with someone.

Cassie staggered back with a gasp, fumbling apologies and hoping no one had been watching her. The few months at The Rocking J ingrained her mind with a mental map of the ranch, but weather and unpaved surfaces were always subject to change and she would forever have to be conscious of her steps.

"I don't think I've ever seen you stumble on someone you or your horse hadn't already sensed was there."

Jake's voice was casual teasing, but Cassie's defenses sharpened with his comment, and she openly glared at him.

"Most people don't stand as quietly as possible in the middle of the road waiting for a blind person to bump into them."

Jake was silent at her angry retort, and her cheeks blushed furiously. She heard him shift uncomfortably from one foot to the other before stepping back from her.

"I'm sorry, Cassie. I wasn't watching to see if you'd bump into me; I was just coming to talk to you about Starlight, and I wasn't thinking."

Cassie grimaced guiltily and tossed her dark hair back from her flushing cheeks. "I'm sorry, Jake. I'm still a little unsteady around here, and you startled me."

"Where is everyone?"

Cassie heard his voice drift from side to side as he looked around the ranch yard.

"If the vans and trucks are gone, then they have already gone to your place for the annual benefit dinner."

Jake was silent, and Cassie narrowed her eyes against the heat of the sun blaring against her left cheek.

"Why would they have gone without you? Are you supposed to be walking the six miles to the ranch?"

Jake's voice held a sharp disapproving edge, and Cassie fought back a smile. It surprised her that he had immediately picked up on the predicament she would be in if all the vehicles were gone and she was not with them. Most people rarely remembered that she could not just jump in her car and go wherever she wanted.

With an unconscious shake of her head, she attempted to fight back the fluttery feeling his response sparked in her. Jake Caswell was not a man to be trusted, she forcefully reminded herself. Everything Debra told her about Jake's past and the times Cassie unintentionally witnessed his genuine goodness had planted seeds of faith in her mind. Seeds that now seemed to be exploding into full foliage on their own accord.

"I'm not going to the fundraiser. Cody is with his grandparents in Reno, and he calls every night at nine. Someone has to be here for the call. He doesn't care who, so I told Miriam I could use the time to catch up on my therapy notes. My screen reading program has been down for a couple of days while I wait for the upgrade."

"Your screen what?"

"My screen reading program," Cassie reiterated. "How do you think I work on the computer?"

Silence met her again, and Cassie pictured Jake's blank expression as he tried to imagine her on a computer. Her laughter broke the stillness of the heavy heat, and Jake began chuckling dark in his chest as well.

"I guess I never thought about it." Jake made the admission sheepishly, but Cassie's ears picked up on a different sound.

"Jake . . . your lungs are still rasping. Have you been to a doctor yet?"

Cassie turned, putting the setting sun behind her again and moved toward the house, Jake trailing her and the dust her stick was kicking up. As he stepped beside and took her elbow in his hand, Cassie automatically pulled her arm free of his grasp and slid her hand to hold his elbow. She fell in one step behind him as they kept walking, her mind registering how naturally she let him take the lead of a sighted guide, and how instinctually he'd done it as if they'd practiced it before.

"I had it checked with the doctor; he says there will be some scarring, and I just need to stay active so I don't lose any of my lung capacity."

Jake stopped at the stairs to the porch, and Cassie dropped her hand from his arm.

"It's a good thing you and your ears aren't around my house. My mom is hypersensitive about every cough and tickle in my throat. If you talked to her about what you hear, I would be in bed around the clock."

"Avoid Caswell Farms until September. Got it," Cassie muttered, trying not to blush guiltily with the reference of talking to his mother.

Cassie felt the blush of her cheeks climb higher as Jake said nothing. She was sure she could feel his eyes watching her face flush; she cleared her throat.

Jake sat down next to her and quietly asked, "Do you think I'll be safe by September?"

"You won't be there anymore starting in September, right?"

She heard the sound of his head moving in response but she couldn't tell if he was nodding or shaking it. Cassie caught a gasp in her throat as she realized she hoped he was going to correct her assumption about September.

"I . . . I have a shoot in New Zealand in September," he answered, "but I also have a proposal for the mustang preserve that I have to file with the Bureau of Federal Land Grants. I have to decide which needs me more."

Jake's deep voice was a little broken, and Cassie responded carefully.

"The way I understood it, you are pretty good at doing both."

Jake leaned back against the steps, and Cassie felt the shift of his body beside her as the wood creaked beneath his weight.

"I guess up until now I have done all right, but this was never the plan."

Cassie could feel a surge of emotion suddenly flow like rushing water. As the sensation passed between them, she knew Jake was ready to give words to what had been haunting him since that fire, and she reclined back against the steps next to him.

"What was the original plan?"

Jake did not respond, and she pictured him staring off into the dusky twilight deciding how much of this he could put words to.

"Five years ago when I got the original grant, it was temporary and based on my ability to make Mustang Mountain a self-contained wildlife preserve. Through the development of the natural resources and the expansion of the herd I have been able to do that, but now . . ."

His voice broke off, and Cassie waited while he brewed over his thoughts before continuing.

"When I was seventeen, it made sense. I was all about those horses, and a life here working with them was all I could see. I had this whole dream of living up at the reservoir and we . . ."

Jake's voice broke off again, and Cassie suddenly had the image of a beautiful girl race into her mind.

"Anyway," he said clearing his throat. "That was before I was doing this acting thing, and now what I originally thought of as my life doesn't look anything like I thought it would. The preserve needs someone to run it full time. There's too much for me and my dad to try to do between our other careers, and I have to decide if I am going to give it up."

"Which one?"

"Which one . . . what?"

"Which one are you worried about giving up?"

Jake didn't answer, and Cassie felt a shift in their formerly comfortable exchange. "Are you happy doing either one?"

Cassie could tell that Jake had not expected her to ask that question, and she waited for him to recover his voice.

"I enjoy different parts of both," he stammered uncomfortably.

Cassie sighed and shook her thick hair away from her face. "Which one holds more pain than you can live with?"

"I don't think I understand. Neither one is painful. They both require hard work, but I can handle that."

Cassie shook her head fiercely and grimaced into the western sky. "No, Jake. No matter which lifestyle we choose, there is pain involved. Whether it's pain over our past, unfulfilled expectations, or regrets about the person we have become. Growth can be painful."

Jake started to chuckle darkly and then gave a short cough. "I don't understand any of that, Cassie. You're the one with the college degree. If you can't put it into real life terms, I'm lost."

Cassie grimaced and bit her bottom lip. Her mind flashed to a mental picture she still carried of Dylan, and she hesitated only momentarily before turning away from Jake.

"Fine, Jake, but after I tell you this real life story, I would appreciate if you'd at least attempt to understand."

Her words were quick and sharp, and the absence of sound from Jake made her take a deep breath and soften her tone.

"Before I came to work with Miriam, I worked in a teen behavioral program in Albuquerque. I absolutely loved it. I loved the work, the ranch, and the kids. It was very fulfilling, and I felt as if I had finally found where I was supposed to be. The couple who ran the program were like my own parents, and the people I worked with were the best group of people I have ever known. The guy I worked the most closely with was a probation officer named Dylan Haskins. He taught me more about behavior modification than I had ever learned. He was amazing with these kids: tough, firm, kind. Loving. And we soon ended up dating and eventually engaged."

Jake shifted uncomfortably beside her, and Cassie took a deep calming breath. She knew this would be more emotional intimacy than Jake was used to, but if he was going to trust her with his past. she was going to have to take a chance on him with hers.

"Dylan and I had only been engaged for about a week when one my boys ran from the program, and I had to pick him up from juvenile detention. When I went to the office to sign him out, one of the female officers was talking about Dylan. She said that even though he was engaged, he didn't let it put a damper on his social life.

She still saw him every Friday night at the bar because that was the night his fiancé was working. After I worked out everything at the detention center, I called Dylan and asked him what was going on."

Cassie stopped again, and Jake sat up from the steps.

"Let me guess, he had some lame excuse, and you could tell he was lying so you quit your job and haven't seen or talked to him since."

"No, Jake," Cassie snapped. "He had himself transferred and sent me an empty box in the mail with a note asking me to send the ring back. He didn't even bother to write the note in Braille so I could read it privately. I had to have one of the people from work read it out loud to me."

Jake fell silent, and Cassie felt the burning of the familiar rage in her chest as she remembered the day Dylan had humiliated her so thoroughly.

"Fine, Jake, skip the story. The point is even after I managed to find out that he had been picking up girls in bars all along, and that I was the only one who didn't know, I forgave him because I wasn't going to let my memories and my past change me in to someone I didn't want to be."

"But you left your job in Albuquerque to get away from him."

Cassie shook her head and turned her face towards him. "No, I didn't. When Miriam called looking for a specialist in mobility for the blind, it was too perfect an opportunity to pass up. I used to believe I would never leave Albuquerque because eventually Dylan would figure out what he had lost, but I learned that losing something or someone is not a place to stand still. It's a drop off into a new reality—cold, brutal, painful. But not as bad as teetering on the edge of a past that has no way to go backward."

Jake stood from the steps now, shuffling discontentedly and shoving his hands into his pockets. "That's different, Cassie, you had a past that might actually come back to you. Mine is gone. Parts of that old reality no longer exist, and if I go into a new reality then I have to just . . ."

Cassie stood and leaned on her cane as Jake broke off and turned his back on her.

"I'll just have to go load that horse, that's all. I'll see ya."

Cassie listened to him walk away and heard the roar of the truck's engine before she turned for the steps and the ranch house. He wasn't going any further with her right now. She sighed as her cane found the screen door.

Chapter Thirteen

"Jake," Natalie's voice tempted. "Why are you out here, alone?"

Jake kept his gaze fixed on the lines of the horses grazing contentedly in the setting sun, the sounds of the benefit dinner rising up behind them. The massive roan stallion dwarfed Starlight's sleek, glossy figure, and he admired the grace of their movements as they nuzzled each other in the pasture.

"What do you want, Natalie? I'm not in the mood tonight."

Natalie lost no time perching her long legs on the top rail of the fence and holding on to Jake's shoulder for balance. "You're missing all the fun," she crooned. "Unless you had something else in mind out here."

Jake stepped away from the whitewashed fence, and Natalie teetered dangerously off balance. Grinning at her he held out his hand, then pulled her down off the top rail.

"Go back to the party, Nat. I'm not going to be any fun tonight."

"You haven't been any fun for a while, Jake. You aren't coming to Mcgoo's much anymore, and I can never find you anywhere except The Rocking J."

"I know. It's been a little crazy since the fire."

Natalie made a face with the mention of the fire, and Jake rubbed his hand over the tender new skin along his jaw.

"I'm glad it wasn't as bad as I heard. People were saying your face melted clear off."

"I was burned, Natalie, but it wasn't that bad."

"That's not what I heard, and I was scared to come look at you like that."

Natalie gave a little shudder and then grinned at Jake's tormented features. "It's gone now, right?"

Jake turned away from her and stared blankly back over the fields. "Yeah, Nat. Something's definitely gone."

Chapter Fourteen

"Jake. What a wasted night." Cassie leaned, exhausted on the doorframe of her studio apartment, listening to the blackness before her.

After Jake's abrupt departure the night before, she had slept restlessly, the sharp edges of old wounds bothering her peace of mind. Summer's intensity was draining enough without the lack of a good night's sleep to worsen the feeling.

Her entire day had been consumed with her clients and Jana's incessant pleadings to accompany her and Lacey to the river party. Silver Creek was swollen with spring runoff, and the local cowboys were taking a shot at wakeboarding from Navajo Canyon Bridge.

Cassie had made no promises, but the prospect of all that water, crowds of unfamiliar voices, and the inevitability of too much alcohol increased her trepidations.

It would be cooler up the canyon, and she could take her laptop and digital voice recorder with her. The girls could swim or flirt or whatever, and she could use her head phones to type up her therapy notes on her computer. Her hand reflexively wrapped around the streaming voice recorder as she listened to the sound of her clock calling out the hour.

Cassie stepped quickly into her apartment, grabbing her laptop bag from her room, and returning to the still-open door. A hot desert breeze brought the smell of creosote and sage along with the sound of Jana's Jeep honking from the foot of the outer staircase.

"Cass, grab your stuff. The sun goes down on the mountain by eight."

*

Locking her door and finding Jana's Jeep had taken no time at all, but Jana drove as if they had lost precious hours of daylight.

"Jana," Cassie said breathlessly. "It's not even six o'clock. Slow down."

Cassie's death grip on the door handle tightened as she felt the car careen around a curve in the dirt road. The energy in the Jeep was charged with expectancy, and Cassie pictured Jana's face squished into grim determination as she hunched over the wheel.

"I know, I know," Jana muttered, not easing off the accelerator. "Dan Collins told me if I came tonight, he would personally teach me to wakeboard. If I'm too late and Natalie Harper and all her bar bunny friends show up in their bikini tops, I will lose my chance to get some one-on-one time with him."

"Dan Collins? I have never heard you talk about him. Who is he?"

The tone of Jana's voice lifted, and Cassie could imagine a wide smile splashed across Jana's dark features now more ruddy in a blush.

"I met him at Mcgoo's a few weeks ago. The old Hudson Dairy went out of business years ago and has been for sale but no one ever thought anyone would buy it."

"And Dan did?" Cassie asked, bracing herself against another too tight turn.

"Dan's uncle. I can't remember his name. He just told Dan if he would come help him make something out of it, the uncle would pay him and eventually will it to him. Evidently the old man is some kind of technology tycoon, and he just bought the place outright and can afford to make it run without profit."

"So that means Dan will be a semi- if not permanent fixture for a while."

Cassie heard the smile on Jana's face again, as her friend's voice brightened.

"That's what he says. I hope he is serious. He is cute and sort of shy, and he has these warm chocolate brown eyes."

Cassie laughed as Jana sighed dreamily but did not ease up on the accelerator.

"He sounds perfect. Hard working, kind, not one of the local boys . . ."

Cassie missed Jana's response as the tires squealed around a corner, and the Jeep's engine roared again.

" . . . It's better to spend time with someone who is not looking for summer romance," she sighed. "These here-today-gone-tomorrow guys get tiring."

Silence drifted between them for a few seconds before Jana quietly asked, "Do you think Jake is going to become permanent after this summer?"

Cassie's chin snapped up too quickly as she turned to face Jana with a glare.

"What difference does it make whether he stays or not?"

"Well, none to some people. Natalie and her friends prefer good time cowboys, and Carter might kill someone if he has to share with Jake year round, but I thought it might matter to you." Cassie shivered at the Carter reference but gave Jana no other response. "Maybe it's none of my business, but you and Jake seem to be . . ."

"What? Friends?"

"Maybe just less of enemies," Jana teased.

Cassie shook her head furiously before she realized it, and then took another shuddered breath.

"Don't get me wrong, Jana, I actually like Jake. He seems like a good guy, a little tortured perhaps, but a good man. Whether he stays on full time or not doesn't matter. What Jake needs is a way to understand himself. He has never defined who he is working to become, so what he does or where he goes to do it is insignificant."

Cassie assumed Jana was nodding her head in understanding as the Jeep pulled to stop beside the rushing water.

Jana's slight hesitation before jumping from the Jeep was only long enough for Cassie to announce she intended to spend some time working.

"Troy is with the bridled mares tied to the willows. And Lacey is by the Dutch ovens, so you can follow your nose to either of them if you get confused, okay?" Jana's voice floated back.

*

Trying to find a quiet place to listen to her notes turned out to be more of a test of her reflexes than anything else. The murky river water had flooded the banks and receded back between the river's shores, leaving a slick black mud behind.

As she plunged her cane into the boggy surface, it was thick and heavy, giving it the texture of stability, but Cassie's flip-flops found only glossy slick surfaces to rest on. And had she not had her cane, she would be covered in the brine.

Finally locating the protruding trunk roots of a weeping willow, Cassie ducked beneath its low hanging branches and rested her back against its trunk. The green wet smell of the river and plants mingled with the pungency of the horses and the cooking dinner. Bursts of laughter, rushing water, and exclamations of triumph as well as defeat greeted her ears, and Cassie smiled contentedly. The sounds became distant and muted as she put in her ear buds, opened her laptop, and pressed the power button to play back her notes on her busy afternoon.

Lost in her sightless world, Cassie worked quickly, typing her notes and recommendations into the laptop. They were too high up on the mountain, and she wouldn't be able to e-mail them to her constituents, but at least she would be ready once they were back in the desert.

Cassie turned off the playback mode of the recorder and was switching it to record to make a verbal note to check on Heidi, when she heard the sound of someone moving across the swampy ground. Pausing the recorder, she listened, and then tightened her grip on the mechanism in her palm as she recognized a familiar voice midst the sounds.

"I haven't seen him here tonight. Are you sure you heard him tell Natalie he was coming?"

Cassie instantly recognized the drunken slur of the voice speaking just beyond the overhanging branches of the tree. The reflexive movement of her fingers taking the recorder off pause clicked alarmingly in her own ears, but remained lost to Carter as he hovered somewhere beyond her quiet spot.

"Maybe he's not here because his little blind friend isn't, either."

"Do you want to go check at Caswell Farms?" asked an unrecognizable voice.

Carter made an ugly grunting sound at his companion, and then swore. "Robert Caswell has a fire investigator out there still. If I randomly show up, Jake might remember that I was the last one in the stalls that day."

Cassie held her breath, afraid that even the sound of her breathing would alert Carter to her presence. She was used to people having quiet conversations around her, forgetting that her ears were particularly sensitive to even slight sounds. She had accidently eavesdropped on more than one conversation when people spoke confidentially to one another, forgetting there was no filter for her ears. That had been how she had learned of Dylan's true intentions; two women quietly gossiping in that detention center, knowing she was Dylan's fiancée, and assuming she could not hear them laugh at her.

Cassie bit down firmly on her bottom lip, grateful this time that Carter was either too drunk or too stupid to look around and notice her. She cautiously placed the recorder in the pocket of her shorts and remained as motionless as possible.

"How long will it take for them to close the arson investigation?"

"Who knows? The sheriff is too stupid to figure it out, and it's not like I left behind proof."

"You don't think Casanova has already pointed the finger at you?"

"It don't matter," Carter said, spitting into the mud. "There's not enough time or money to prove anything. No matter what Jake tells them, unless I tell them I set the fire, they've got no proof it was me."

Carter's drunken laughter at his cruel statement became background clutter as Cassie's pulse began pounding in her ears.

Carter had tried to kill Jake. The brutality of the thought sent a shiver of dread across her shoulders.

Carter and his drinking buddy laughed as casually as if they had been discussing the weather. As the two men's conversation drifted to their plans to hit Mcgoo's if Jake did not appear, Cassie remembered her still running voice recorder and ended the verbal note. She waited, a little breathless, beneath the willows until the voices moved away before she rose, took a few faltering steps, and then pushed the willows aside.

The pungent odors of the party mixed with the river cleared her tumbling thoughts for a moment, and she suddenly caught the scent of alcohol, sweat, and cattle.

Pausing to tilt her nose toward the smell, Cassie's nerves tightened, as she heard a curse of realization directly in front of her.

Cassie held her white cane in her right hand and wrapped the fingers of her left slowly around the handle.

"Have you been hiding under that tree all night?" Carter hissed. Cassie stepped back and braced her feet in the mud. "No wonder Diego and I couldn't find you. You got Jake hidden around here somewhere, too. You his guardian angel now?"

The bitter sneer in the man's voice made Cassie flinch internally, and she wondered if the expression had crossed her face.

"I haven't been hiding, Carter, just working." Cassie was tempted to let go of her cane long enough to open her laptop case and show him her computer, slung behind her, but the feeling of treachery clinging to this exchange prompted her to leave her hands grasping the only weapon she owned.

Carter made a wet noise in his throat, and she felt his body heat drawing nearer. The intensity of the moment was shattered as a computerized voice announced. "The voice recorder is now off."

Carter's motion halted, as if the sound had chained his will to move. Cassie's breath shuddered in her chest, and Carter swore again.

"Give me that recorder," he commanded.

For a man bogged down in beer and mud, Carter moved incredibly fast. He was on her in a fracture of a second, grabbing her shoulders and growling his foul breath into her face. If he hadn't been so close to her, she knew he could have seen the flash of her stark white cane coming toward him as she levered it upward and smashed it between his legs. His grip tightened and he howled, but he did not let go.

"You'll pay for that, you little . . ." Before the words had slid from his forked tongue, Cassie screamed.

The sounds of panic tumbled all around her as if she were immersed in a waterfall of noises. The horses stomped and snorted, voices, footsteps, and shouts erupted all around her and Carter.

She smiled. "If I were you I would step back."

The barrage of questions and concerns piled all around them as the partygoers showed up to the commotion.

Carter was mostly silent in the interrogation as Cassie reassured Jana and Troy that she had just slipped in the mud, and Carter had caught the end of her stick before she fell. He had complained loudly, and she was startled with his presence. It was just a misunderstanding. She waited for Carter to slink away somewhere as soon as possible.

She wanted to check the recording and make sure the unintentional confession had been captured by the device, but Carter was ever-present. She should have told them he had attacked her, but she needed to get that recording to someone safely, and she was almost sure Carter's diligence in staying was meant to prevent that from happening.

She finally got away from him on their return through Navajo Canyon, but Jana took a couple of other girls back with her and there was no chance for Cassie to listen to her notes.

*

After saying goodnight to the others and locking herself in her apartment, Cassie listened to her notes for the day. She wasn't sure if the bit of broken conversation she had would be enough to arrest Carter, but if she gave it to Jake, he would at least be able to watch more carefully.

After downloading the recordings from her sim card, Cassie put the card in a zipper bag, sliding it between the phone books Miriam put in the kitchen drawer. A part of her rushing emotion had been quelled as she focused on the monotony of what needed to be done. In the quiet of her apartment and the hum of far off crickets, the tears now flowed.

Cassie took a towel from the countertop and pressed it into her mouth as she sobbed. She knew her reaction disproportionate to the circumstances, but she did not try to dam it. Open wounds from Dylan, the fluctuating emotions that Jake aroused in her, and now this. It was too much. Nothing had happened with Carter tonight, at least not much. The knowledge that she was somehow caught up in Jake's tragic past could have made her angry. She wanted to feel vindicated; he deserved to be plagued for his reputation. That's what her mind said. Although, deep in her heart, she felt none of that when she heard the truth about the fire. She didn't believe Jake deserved any of this, Casanova or not.

Chapter Fifteen

"Congratulations, Jake," he muttered bitterly to himself while pulling the truck over next to the white rail fence outside The Rocking J.

He wasn't sure how he had ended up back here. He had purposely been avoiding The Rocking J for the last couple of days. Tonight, though, Cassie was finished with work and waiting for him in the ranch house. She told him over the phone that she wanted to give him something, and now that he was here, his heart pounded, leaving him anxious and sweating.

It didn't seem like such a good idea. This was the only time she had ever called him. They all called, eventually, no matter how shy or uninterested they pretended to be, all the girls who knew him called him about dancing, or going out. Now she had . . .

He wondered for the thousandth time what he was doing. She called him, and he came running. He couldn't tell if he felt triumphant with her request for him to come over, or if he was dreading the possibility that Cassie was just like all the others. Waning confidence and dying pride told him to pull himself together and feel victorious. He had won. Jolts of bitter anger argued that claim. He had won nothing.

He could see the lemon yellow light from the apartment above the garage and the movement of a shadowed figure in the light. He couldn't convince himself not to watch her moving behind the curtains. He would just watch for a moment, and then he would get it over with.

The bulky shadow registered in Jake's mind suddenly. The shoulders were too broad, the waist and torso too thick to be Cassie. Maybe she had a date in the apartment with her. That thought was almost more painful than his previous ones, and Jake swore.

Jake shook his head. His thoughts were getting out of control. Of course it was her. That explanation only created new questions, though. Why did she have a light on? It would have made no difference to her.

As Jake watched, the light turned off, and the door to her apartment opened.

Carter Langdon's face glowed briefly in the moonlight as he descended the staircase next to the garage, and then disappeared into the alfalfa field beyond the house.

Jake sat stunned. His previous wonderings about Cassie's visitor resurfaced as his mind tried to make sense of what he had just seen. Carter was in Cassie's apartment? Was she going out with Carter? Did she even know Carter's voice well enough to know that he was trouble? Jake's stampeding thoughts became hobbled as he realized Cassie knew nothing of his history with the Langdons or why she shouldn't trust Carter.

A new feeling of protectiveness washed over him, and he jumped from his truck and ran the length of the driveway toward the wooden staircase. Determined to fill her in on the truth of her predicament with Carter, Jake was halfway up the stairs when Cassie's voice stopped him.

"I called the sheriff's department. You had better get out of here or be prepared to answer questions about what you're doing breaking into my house."

"Cassie? I thought you were up there. It's Jake."

"Jake!" Cassie snapped. "Why are you prowling around in my apartment? I told you to meet me down here."

"No, Cass. I just got here. I thought you were upstairs with a . . . date . . . or something."

The color drained from Cassie's tan, and Jake moved quickly to her side. Her lips quivered only slightly, but he could feel her reaction to the information as he laid his hands on her arms.

"Did you really call the sheriff? You look terrified."

"I haven't called yet, but all I have to do is press send and the call will go out."

"You look like you want to make that call. What's wrong?"

Cassie took a shuddered breath and filled Jake in on the party the night before. Pulling her voice recorder out of her pocket, she played back the overheard conversation between Carter and his friend.

"That's why I called you to come over tonight. I don't know if it's enough or even if you want to do anything about it, but I thought you should at least have it."

Jake was nodding without realizing she couldn't see it.

Cassie impatiently asked, "Jake? Why does this guy want you dead? Why aren't you calling the police yourself? I think he's dangerous."

"It's not that simple, Cassie. This is a very small, very old town. The Langdons are well known. Carter and his problems are well known, but everyone just sort of ignores him. The sheriff is his uncle for hell's sake. And ever since high school, I have been an outsider."

"I understand all that, Jake, I'm not trying to step on small-town politics, but he set fire to your corrals knowing you were inside. That's a little more serious than just drinking too much and needing to sleep it off."

Jake shuffled his feet distractedly. He was listening to her but her words were needling the back of his mind. The surer she sounded about Carter being dangerous, the more the other guy's presence that night worried Jake.

"I hate to interrupt your righteous indignation, and I appreciate your concern for me. I really do. I think you should ask yourself what he was doing in your apartment, though."

Cassie turned for the staircase, and Jake took her hand firmly.

"I think you should stay here and press the send button. Let me go find out what's going on upstairs."

"Jake, I can't . . . I don't think . . ."

He could hear in her voice she was amenable to this plan, and her attempt at bravery caused him to reach out and pull her against him.

"Make the call for me, please," he whispered into her hair. "I'm not sure I'll survive another fire or worse if he booby-trapped your house. Stay here. I'll be right back."

*

Vaulting the steps two at a time and bursting open the door to Cassie's apartment, Jake only half heard Cassie speak to the dispatcher on her phone. When a firebomb didn't greet Jake's appearance in the small room, Jake breathed easier. Reaching out his hand for the light switch, Jake felt around for the uneven surface, listening intently. The room remained dark as he felt around, but his undisguised movements brought a distinct sound. He heard the threat long before he flipped the lights on and saw the snake coiled and rattling in the center of Cassie's floor.

The copperhead and diamond pattern of the reptilian body was six feet long. Its tail vibrated in clear annoyance, and its black eyes glimmered at Jake, frozen outside the door. The diamondback rattler drew its head back to strike, and Jake felt the shock of seeing it push him further back onto the landing. It moved fast, its long, dripping teeth imbedding themselves into the linoleum at the apartment's entrance. As the viper pulled itself into another coil, Jake reached for the knob and slammed the fiberglass door between them.

Jake collapsed onto the top step of the landing, breathing deeply and waiting for the buzz of adrenaline to clear from his blood. The hiss and slither of reptilian scales across the linoleum behind her door made his skin crawl as he closed his eyes and heard what she would have.

The creeping sensation in his flesh vanished as he heard the sound of screeching tires and screaming sirens racing down the driveway into the ranch yard. Jake stood quivering in the flashing lights of the county sheriff's car.

"Jake?" Ed Harris's voice boomed. "What are you doing, son?"

Jake took a deep breath as he heard the hiss of the snake beyond the doorway and then descended the stairs to meet Ed's calloused features.

"Miss Taylor reported a prowler and when I get here, you are breaking in to her residence. You want to explain yourself?"

Jake saw Cassie step from the doorway of the ranch house with the ever present calm on her face. As he explained what he had seen to Sheriff Harris, Cassie moved down the stairs to listen to his description. As he spoke of the sound that had first caught his attention, Cassie gasped and unconsciously stepped back from where he was talking quietly. He had kept his voice low in hopes of sparing her too many details, but she had heard every word. Now, the panic he saw earlier in her pale blue eyes was replaced with sheer terror, and Jake could only imagine the fear of walking into a room to hear that sound and be helpless to know where the attack would come from.

Jake unconsciously reached out and took her hand firmly in his, attempting to reassure them both. She explained Jake's presence to the deputy's, and Jake moved his arm around her shoulders, not sure her knees would keep her upright. As the two officers emerged with a rough cloth sack, they reported the specifics of the incident to the sheriff as quietly and confidentially as possible, but Jake could see by the look on her face she heard every grizzly word of the sprung trap that had been set for her.

They had cut off the snake's head, killing it, and removed its body. It now lay in an empty burlap bag in the bed of the sheriff's truck.

Jake was thankful Cassie did not have the ability to watch what happened. Color had not yet returned to her cheeks, and the sight of the burlap sack was giving him the creeps. Cole Butler, one of the deputies, walked awkwardly to their grouping and whistled under his breath. He shot a doubtful look at Jake, followed by an apologetic smile before returning to the sheriff's truck.

"Jake, there's no sign of Carter or anyone else here tonight." Sheriff Harris' voice snapped his attention back. "It's dark out tonight, and you said yourself you only saw his face in the moonlight. Considering your history with the Langdons, is it possible you only thought it was Carter?"

Jake stared dumbfounded for a moment, then glanced at Cassie. She was scowling suspiciously as well, but not at him. Her open mistrust was focused on the sheriff's careful questioning, and Jake automatically stood a little straighter. If his words had wound strength and structure into Cassie's body, she would share it with him now. Standing their ground, she pulled away from his arm around her, and Jake crossed them over his chest.

"It was him. Like you said I've got a history with that guy. I would not mistake him," he said firmly.

Sheriff Harris mumbled something about tracking Carter down and questioning him, but both Cassie and Jake knew it would just be a formality. There was no proof of anything except that someone had pulled a cruel and dangerous prank on her, and there was nothing left to do about it.

After the police retreated back down the driveway, Cassie and Jake stood motionless before the dark ranch house. The hot, sticky breeze blew the wind chimes hanging from the covered porch, and Jake took Cassie's hand and began walking with her back up the driveway. She pulled her fingers from his and slid her hand up to the crook of his arm, gently wrapping her hand around his bicep just above the elbow. Falling in step one stride behind him, Cassie followed Jake as he moved silently through the night.

"Where is everyone tonight?" Jake asked.

"Miriam went to Reno to pick up Cody at his grandparents', and you know how it goes. When the cats away, the mice get dates and party till the sun comes up," Cassie said.

"Did your date ditch out on you tonight, or you just don't party with the sighted after last night?"

"The sighted were actually very helpful last night." Cassie murmured quietly. "And you know my reasons for not dating."

Jake stopped abruptly, and Cassie bumped into him as he turned to face her.

"One guy turns out to be a loser and all men are out of the picture? That doesn't sound like a very healthy attitude, especially for a therapist."

"I haven't given up on men, Jake. I am taking some time to fix my picker."

Jake turned and began walking again, and Cassie held tightly to his arm. "What's your picker?"

"Most people choose their romantic interests in one of two ways: what they are attracted to physically and what they are attracted to emotionally. Good relationships are combinations of both of those, but the initial attraction is usually the most powerful."

"What does that have to do with your picker?"

"I don't have the ability to be physically attracted to someone immediately, and the emotional attraction with Dylan totally led me astray. Evidently, I am not very good at picking out appropriate, trustworthy mates based on the emotional, and I can't do it with my sight, so . . . "

Her words trailed off, and Jake paused at the bottom step on her staircase. As he turned to face her again, Cassie put both of her hands out and felt around until she grabbed the rail leading up to her apartment. Instant recognition flooded her expression and the grim, lines at the edges of her mouth vanished.

"I guess I never thought about where attraction really comes from." Jake said leaning against the opposite rail. "I'm not attracted to every woman I see, but it is usually what I see that catches my attention."

"That's because men love what they are attracted to, and women are attracted to what they love. Women have had to catch the eye of their pursuers since the beginning of time. Men, on the other hand, need things like status, money, or influence to woo their mates."

Jake took a wayward lock of Cassie's hair and tucked it behind her ear. "What was it that Dylan had?"

"Dylan had words; words that sounded like poetry and music. I misunderstood charm for sincerity. I am trying to learn how to tell insincerity from genuine goodness."

Jake felt his cheeks grow hot and was immediately grateful that she could not see it. He didn't need to mentally review his behavior with women and more specifically with her to know she was talking about him.

Cassie cleared her throat roughly, and Jake's attention snapped back, "I'm sorry, Jake. I never intended for you to take that personally. I can feel how awkward this topic has gotten for you, so I'll drop it. Just know . . . you are one of the reasons I think my picker is broken. You have not turned out to be exactly what I thought you were, and my confidence where guys are concerned is a little unsteady."

Jake laughed, despite the sting he felt at her words. He grappled for a way to turn this exchange more comfortable. "The sheriff assured me you are perfectly safe in your apartment tonight, but I got the feeling you don't trust him much either. Are you going to be okay?"

"I see what you mean about small-town politics, but I'd have felt better if you let him hear the recording."

"It wouldn't be proof of Carter's presence here tonight. All we know, for sure, is that Carter strongly suspects you recorded him. Ed will believe nothing but hard proof, and we don't have that yet."

"There's something else, Jake. I can hear it in your voice. You aren't sure you want to get Carter in trouble."

"Oh, I don't mind Carter getting what he deserves. I guess I just wonder how much of that I should feel guilty about. Plus, I don't want to bring any more of Carter's focus to you. He and I were friends a long time ago. If I talk to him, he might just need to hit me, and then no one else has to get hurt."

"First of all, I think it's too late for that. Second, you cannot blame yourself for Carter's present troubles, no matter what role you played in his past."

Cassie's voice was too blunt on his conscience, especially when she turned her arctic eyes on him. "What do you have to feel guilty about?"

"A lot, actually. Too much . . ."

Jake ran his hands absentmindedly through his hair, drawing away from this topic of conversation. She seemed to sense his reluctance and took his elbow again, turning him toward the ascending stairs. "Jake, could I ask you for a favor? I'm sure those cops took care of that snake but could you go up and see if there is anything or anyone up there that I should know about?"

Jake grimaced, removed her hand from his arm, and held it firmly. "I appreciate the vote of confidence Cass, but you're coming, too."

Chapter Sixteen

"Jake," Cassie whispered from the doorway of her apartment. "Is it safe?"

She heard the slight scrape of his boots on the carpet, and her heart automatically seized with the sound.

"Cassie, unless I am moving in or you're moving out, you've got to come make sure yourself. Take my hand," he said softly. "I'll talk you through it."

Jake kept up a running commentary as they inspected every corner of the small studio apartment. He explained in great detail where everything was located, and she affirmed nothing had been disturbed. He offered to empty her laundry basket onto the floor to check the bottom, but Cassie blushed and told him she could dig through her laundry herself.

After both she and Jake were satisfied with the search, she heard him sink onto her small love seat. Cassie folded her long legs crisscross beneath her and sat on the floor at his feet.

"Thank you for the verbal tour. It helped a lot. I may even be able to sleep here alone tonight."

Jake was silent before her, and she heard the sound of a yawn escaping involuntarily. "It's late and I'm fine if you want to go, it's just that I'm finding the sound of your voice very . . ." Cassie broke off thoughtfully before she found the description she was looking for. "I find it very . . . giant redwood."

"Very what? Did you just say my voice sounds like a tree's voice? I know my ears aren't as good as yours, but I am pretty sure trees don't have voices."

"Not sounds like a tree. Feels like a tree."

"That's actually less helpful. I don't know how a tree feels either, or how it compares to a voice."

Cassie laughed ruefully. How could she explain this to him? A sighted person's world was filled with so many colors and images, she wasn't sure she could make sense of this for him.

"No, Jake, just listen. If you go to a redwood forest in California, it feels like strength. The smell is of ancient earth and wood. The sounds are of hushed reverence. The air is steady, warm, like your favorite blanket wrapped around you." She paused listening for his response, but he was quiet. "The sound of your voice, here in a room full of questions, feels like those trees."

"Cassie, do you have any memories of what things look like?"

The question was so sidelong that Cassie thought she could feel its weight on her cheeks. He was asking her more than what she remembered from her sighted life. He was asking her to bring him into her present one.

"I have flashes of shapes, light, shadow. It's kind of like waking up from a dream and only grasping at the memory of what it had been."

"Do you have dreams?"

"Of course I do."

"Do you dream in picture, or just sounds and smells? Do blind people have dreams like regular people?"

Cassie laughed, and she heard him move down onto the floor in front of her, taking her hands in his. "If I let you touch my face, will you see me in your dreams?"

Cassie yanked her hands out of his and folded them in her lap.

"Yes, Jake, blind people dream. For me, I dream in pictures. I don't know how accurate those pictures are, but I see in my dreams."

"What about a person who has never had their sight. Do they dream like that?"

"I don't know, Jake. What makes you so sure that *you* dream like regular people?"

Cassie stiffened as Jake leaned toward her and gently took her hands again. She felt her fingers tremble in his grasp, but she did not pull back from him this time. "What are you doing, Jake?"

"What do you see in your mind when you look at me?"

Cassie felt his eyes watching her reactions. Truthfully, she hadn't formed a picture in her thoughts; she was avoiding that. The more she let her guard down with him, the more difficult it was to trust her judgment. She had not formed concrete impressions of him on purpose. It was easier to forget when he was gone, if she never really looked at him.

When she didn't answer him, he pressed her further. "Do you imagine what color someone's eyes are, or their hair? Do you see something if I tell you my eyes are blue, but not blue like yours?"

"Jake, colors to me are associated with sounds, textures, and smells, not words like blue. I don't know what that means."

She could feel her temper rising with his probing, and the emotion felt more like panic than annoyance. He was too close; she needed the protection he offered her more than she needed his face in her mind tonight. She had to escape.

"It's not something I can explain."

"Try, please. I really want to know. Which is more powerful? Texture? Sound? Or smell?"

When he started rubbing the backs of her hand with his thumbs, she broke free of his calloused fingers and brushed her hair back from her face. If he was going to push, then she would make him see things he didn't want to.

"Texture leaves the strongest impression. For example, my complexion is fairly smooth, but when I was 11 years old I ran into a wooden post that was part of my father's library. The carved edge of the post creased my forehead, and now I have a deep gash that feels to me like the Grand Canyon when I run my fingers over it."

She lowered her head and pointed out the scar to him. Jake's fingers slid lightly over the spot, and a part of her flinched as she felt the edges of the indention graze his skin.

"Cassie, I can't see it, and I don't feel anything either. There's no scar, you are . . ." Jake's voice faltered only momentarily before he lightly traced the edges of her features with his fingertips. "Do you remember that day we were all at the reservoir? I watched you on the dock before you went swimming. The sun was setting behind you and you were beautiful. Your lips, your eyes, your face. I've never seen anything more extraordinary."

Cassie felt her lips involuntarily part as his fingers brushed over them, and she fought the urge to reach out and touch his. The soft, sultry murmur of his words pierced her, and she wanted him to keep his hands on her. "No face is perfect," he teased reluctantly. "I'm sure you could find flaws in mine, if you looked."

With the change in the tenor of his voice, Cassie reclaimed her senses, and leaned backward on her elbows. "Well, that's what I mean; to me I am disfigured by that scar, and I picture it slashing across my forehead obnoxiously. I have no idea what the rest of my face looks like. I've been told I have a creamy complexion, pale blue eyes and auburn hair, but I don't know what that means. What I know is my forehead has a giant crease in it."

"I thought appearance didn't matter to you," he said in a terse retort. "What difference does it make if you have a scar?"

"Why are you so interested in this?" she snapped. "An old friend of yours is trying to kill you, and now me, and you want to talk about what people look like? I think you should tell me what happened in your past with Carter that makes him homicidal and you deserving of such hatred."

Jake's body moved away from her until she heard his voice drifting from his position, reclined on the floor beside her. "If we talk about Carter, then we have to talk about the past," he mumbled. "I don't like talking about the past. It has nothing to do with the present, and it's awkward."

Cassie tried not to smile at him but lost the struggle as she cleared her throat uncomfortably.

"If it has nothing to do with the present, then why is it so hard to talk about?"

"It was painful enough then, why make it worse by feeling it again?"

"Jake, strong feelings that are buried alive never die. Talking about them gives them their last breath before they fade into memories."

"How many breaths have you given your memories of your ex- fiancé? Because it looks to me like every time you talk about it, you are just breathing new life into the pain, not letting it die."

Cassie felt the corners of her mouth turn up sardonically as she stared deeper into his turmoil.

"It gets easier and easier to talk about Dylan without the emotion, and just see it for what it was. I trusted his charm, his sincerity, and his tenderness. I had never experienced a relationship before where I was so close to someone and I couldn't trust their words. Blind people are very honest with each other because trust is such a large part of what we do for survival. Aside from my family and the people at the blind schools, I had little interaction with people who didn't understand that. The cruel or insecure ones either avoid you or attack. You know who and what they are. Dylan was my first experience with someone who lied to me with such beautiful words."

"No wonder you weren't so friendly that night at Mcgoo's. I must have sounded like another Dylan." Cassie felt the air around them ignite with his confession. A part of her wanted to soothe it away, make a joke to break the feeling, but Jake kept talking. "I wasn't like that before I was famous. I was actually pretty oblivious to my own charms before . . ." Jake broke off, and Cassie felt the name clinging to the air between them.

"Before your girlfriend was killed."

His previously relaxed form stiffened beside her, and Cassie kept her features placid while he recovered. "How did you . . . who told you about that?"

"Your mom was worried that the stable fire had brought that pain filled past of yours out from where you had buried it, and she thought maybe I could help."

"Help?" Jake snapped irritably. "Help by telling me some lame story about your own tragic past. Is any of that even true or were you just trying to get me to feel like you understand what it's like to be hurt?"

Cassie closed her eyes and shook her head before gripping her knees tightly.

"No, Jake. I don't talk about Dylan to very many people because it shows my weakness and makes me vulnerable. I trusted you with that part of me because I wanted you to know I could be trusted." Cassie took a deep breath and she heard Jake moving back toward the love seat. "Jake, think about it. What's worse, the memories of a girl you loved who will always love you, no matter what? Or knowing the person you loved and trusted is out there somewhere, choosing not to want or love you anymore? You see this loss as a great tragedy, which it was. But in your world you are still loved, wanted, strong, and heroic. In mine, I am a silly woman who fell for pretty promises and a nice body, but missed what a snake he was."

Cassie sensed the pause in his escape, and the need he had to fight the truth of her words with every tortured syllable. Scrambling to her hands and knees, she went to where he sat, placing her hands on his knees. "Jake, her ghost is haunting you into being a ghost of yourself. This Casanova character that everybody thinks you are is not the man Melinda loved in the first place. You buried him beside her, and now you're holding onto the pain of your past to keep from letting him live again."

Jake's body surrendered, defeated into the cushions of the love seat. Cassie heard his voice muffled as if he held his face in his hands. "Cassie. Why couldn't you be like all the others? Accept the good-time Casanova. Don't look beyond the smile and charm. Why is it so damn easy to let go with you?" he whispered huskily. "Melinda was not in love with me. She wanted the Hollywood actor all along."

Cassie was silent, but her hand still rested on his knee and she held it more tightly.

"Melinda was beautiful, smart, and driven. She was too good for this one-horse town and, more than anything else, she wanted out. The night of the accident we had been arguing about the land grant. I was going to the federal courthouse in Carson City to file the paperwork the next week, and I had turned down a secondary part in a local movie that was shooting in the mountains."

Jake's voice was no longer distorted, and Cassie figured he had moved his hands out of his face. She reached out and took one of them, expecting him to pull away. His fingers tightened convulsively around hers, and she took a ragged breath.

"It was a graduation party and there was a lot of drinking and partying, but Melinda and I spent the whole night fighting. She told me if I didn't give up this horse ranch business and take that part, she was breaking up with me. She said that my face was her best shot at a real life and she wasn't going to shackle herself to Lindley because I was hung up on horses." Jake's voice had become distant with his memories, and Cassie imagined him picturing Melinda that night.

"I was shocked. I mean, I knew I didn't look like Cousin It or anything, but I had never considered a life or career based on my looks until that night. When she started to leave with her brother, I knew he'd been drinking, I didn't know he was drunk, though. Everyone assumed I had gone along to save Melinda from Carter, but the truth is . . . I was afraid if she left that night, I would be forced to choose between her and the mustangs. I went along so I could convince her that the life I had planned on the mountain, with her, was the best for both of us.

"She ignored me for most of the drive, and when the truck rolled off the road that night I was still trying to convince her that my skills as an actor and model were worthless compared to what I could do here. I couldn't save her, and getting Carter out of there only forced him to live with the loss of his sister, the blame for the accident, and the end of his dreams. Melinda was not the only one we lost that night. There were two casualties in that crash."

"Three, Jake. There were three."

Taking a deep breath, he leaned back.

"I was untouched that night, Cassie. The only casualty for me is keeping both her version of me and my version of myself fused for all these years so I can prove to her we could have had it all. Casanova keeps my relationships casual, easy, and I don't have to think about the fact that the man I want to be wasn't good enough for Melinda; that I will never be good enough for anything except Hollywood."

Cassie was kneeling in front of him, and now she slid into the narrow gap to lean against his body. Jake shifted beside her and Cassie turned, placing her hands against his chest and sliding her palms until she touched his neck and jaw.

"I don't know what you look like Jake, or whether your looks have anything to do with who you are, but I am fairly certain I have never pictured this Casanova. Men who can hide behind good looks don't usually understand themselves well enough to care whether there is more that people might be interested in."

Cassie took a shuddered breath, as his hands found her waist and slid onto her back. "I don't care what you look like. I don't care what those other people see, if you will trust me, I can tell you what I feel."

Cassie trailed her fingers over the planes of his features, placed her hands on either side of his face, until she ran her fingers through his silky hair and felt it curl beneath her nails. She pulled it gently between her fingers and her mind formed a picture.

"When I was so sick all those years ago, my grandmother would sit beside me in the hospital doing cross stitch. I couldn't see what picture she was making, the colors she used or the stitch she sewed. However, I could feel the tangled threads curling and silken on the back of the pattern. It was a beautiful picture in my sightless eyes, and your hair feels the same way. What color is it?"

"Black . . . embroidery thread."

Cassie smiled widely. "You're catching on."

She trailed her fingers from his hair to the line of his jaw, and the rough texture of his five o'clock shadow scraped against her fingertips. She touched his jaw, his neck, his chin, and finally ran her fingers over the curve of his mouth. "The country farm where I first learned to ride horses also had a huge sow that had piglets every spring. When piglets are born they have a soft layer of hair that covers their bodies. After three or four days it turns as rough as steel wool, but for those few days it feels like this."

Jake's hand was covering hers now, pressing it against his cheek and catching her breath in her throat.

"This feels like a baby pig to you?" he murmured, his mouth brushing her palm. "I can do better than that."

Cassie felt his fingers wind into her hair and trail teasingly down the back of her neck.

"The first time you ride a wild mustang, she is jittery, full of energy, ready to run." Jake pulled Cassie flush against his body, and she felt the pound of his heart as he whispered in her ear. "There is no time to think, or plan. You must wind your fingers through her mane, and take her. Like the wild thing she is."

His last words were hot against her lips, and she closed her eyes to feel his mouth on hers. The firmness of a peach mixed with the taste of cool water lit like sparks on her tongue. The feeling of the redwoods enveloped her, and she knew she would dream of him tonight.

Chapter Seventeen

"Jake!" Cassie finally gasped. "Slow down. I need to think, and I can't do that clearly when you're kissing me."

Jake felt Cassie pulling away from him and reclaimed her mouth before she could go. He held her against him, his heart pounding with hers like the thunder of horses' hooves racing through his soul. He was alive again, alive in ways he had not felt for so long he had nearly forgotten the sensation. She pulled away again, and he buried his face into her long hair. She smelled of sunshine and alfalfa, and for an instant he saw her without his eyes. She was the touch of the wind against his sunburned neck. She was the taste of chocolate, seasoned beef, and melted cheese. She was the night sky, too vast and deep to understand.

"I thought thinking was what we were avoiding," he teased.

"Maybe that's the problem."

Jake leaned away from her body to look into her fathomless eyes. "This is the first time in a long time I could do that without thinking. It was always a game before, how far to bring them in, how much to hold back, the perfect moment to let go. I have nothing left to hold back, Cassie. I'm not playing, and I don't want to let you go."

"I want to trust you Jake, and I have. But the sun will still rise in the morning, and I need to know if I can face it with more than my name on Casanova's list of conquests. If you wanted to prove that I could be had like all the others, then consider me conquered. It doesn't need to go any further than this; I can live with this."

Jake felt as if the print of her hand were burning across his face. Had she been using him? Was this her way of getting back at

Dylan? Anger stirred inside him and he gritted his teeth before he could say something he would regret.

The expression on her face hid nothing though, and the tears brimming her eyes could not lie. He understood then, her vulnerability, she only had words, touches and feelings to rely on. Her heart didn't know how to see truth in someone's eyes or deceit in the expression of a face. He owed her more than just kisses and promises. He owed her unshakeable trust. She had given it to him, more than if she had offered him her body, she had let him in to her circle of trust and after Dylan had damaged it, she could not afford another breech.

"You're right," he said, trailing a line of kisses from her lips to her ear. "Not about putting you on Casanova's list, but about slowing down. You need to know that I'm not just here tonight, but every night for however long you want me."

"Those are easy words while we are still here like this, Jake. Tomorrow we have some serious problems and questions that have to be answered."

Jake didn't want to think about any of that. The sudden infiltration of reality between them was bringing up her walls as well as his. Trying to focus on what she wanted, Jake sighed and leaned back into the cushions. "Let's answer some of those questions tonight. Maybe if I can make the world go away again, you'll come back to me the way you were before."

"How's that?" Cassie whispered.

"Lost in what works instead of fixing what doesn't."

"It's the survivor in me, Jake. I die if I focus on what feels good, but doesn't work."

"This," he enunciated, pulling her to rest against him, "feels good and it works."

"What about the rest?"

Jake ran his fingers through his hair as Cassie reached up and touched his face.

"You look worried," she said.

"Not worried, just thinking. If I go home now, I'll be back tomorrow after or maybe before I take care of the northwest alfalfa field. We can figure out how to get that recording to the arson investigator. It might be an illegal recording, but at least it will give them a direction to go. I'm going to go let my folks know what is going on, too, so they can watch out at the farm for Carter, and I can be here doing the same."

"Jake, you just can't hang around here and guard me. Miriam will know there's a problem, Cody will come apart, and the entire program will suffer."

She had her head laid against his shoulder and her breath was grazing the base of his throat. "Would you be willing to come stay at my place with my mom and my sister? We can bring Jackpot over, too, and you should be safe enough at Caswell Farms and at work in between."

"Whoa, slow down. I don't need to move anywhere. If I am working and it's safe, then living here is exactly the same. I have managed on my own for most of my life, Jake, and now you want me to hide and cower behind your mom's skirts? I'm not doing that."

Jake grinned at her, and he could have sworn she could see the look on his face. Somehow in the midst of reconfiguring her life and her refusals to cooperate, she had moved to the center of the room and was now glaring at him.

"Cassie," he said cautiously, "the only way Carter will leave you out of this is if I confront him with that recorder. I don't know how long it will take me to find him and work this out. In the meantime, I would feel better if you were . . . under supervision."

"And who exactly do you have in mind for this job? I know for a fact it is not amongst Casanova's skill set."

"No, but it is in *mine*," he said taking her in his arms again. "I won't give you false promises about how you'll never be alone again, but I need you to take me seriously. I will call Carter in the morning and tell him to meet me about the recording. Tonight, though, you should come with me."

Murmuring assurances against her lips, Jake felt her melt into his kisses. The rush of emotion he felt in her arms cleared his thoughts, and Jake used his other senses to explore the sensation. Closing his eyes, he listened to the sound of their broken breaths, tasted the sweetness of her mouth, and touched the curve of her body against his. Tangling his fingers through her hair, he sank back down onto her love seat once more.

The night sprawled silent beyond their embrace, until Jake's lesser instincts finally broke to the surface as Cassie stroked his jaw and spoke. "I'm not moving in with you."

"Not even if it makes it easier for us to do more of this?"

"Not even then, Jake. As much as I'd like a good reason to keep you with me all the time. Your house comes with chaperones."

Jake opened his eyes to look at her. She was teasing him away from his guard dog duties, and this argument was actually working.

"Fine. Can I borrow a pillow at least? This couch thing of yours is going to be hard enough to try and sleep on."

The pillow was found, but unnecessary. Neither he nor Cassie did much sleeping that night. Dawn slipped her amber fingers through the blinds before Jake could persuade Cassie that she couldn't be left alone that night, and Cassie convinced him that she didn't want to be. Sleep simply wasn't on either of their agendas.

When Cassie unwound herself from Jake's arms to take a shower, he paced impatiently, made a few phone calls, and then went to the barn with her before leaving.

*

"Be careful, Jake. Once Carter knows you have that recording, he'll be coming for you."

"That won't happen for a while. I called his place, and he wasn't there. Jana said you've got a client this morning, and Troy is working with you for the rest of the day so he won't come here. If I find him,

I'll call you in case he's gunning for me. If I don't get back here before 2 p.m., call Sheriff Harris and tell him I'm on the northwest field in my dad's truck. Play that message for him and send him to look for me."

"Jake, just call him from here," Cassie said grabbing his arms and clinging to him. "Don't leave and give him the chance to do something like burn you out of the stables again."

"I've got to handle the water on that field or we will lose the whole crop. Carter doesn't know I'm looking for him yet, and when he finds out I will be back here."

"Then why give me a backup plan if you don't come back?"

Her voice had dropped to a whisper, and Jake lifted her chin and kissed her. "So you will know where I am if you want to ditch out on work today and come roll in the alfalfa with me."

"You don't really think that makes me feel better, do you?"

"I can see that it does," he teased, "not to mention that now you're tempted to take me up on the offer."

"Make no mistake about it, Jake Caswell. If you don't come back here, I will hunt you down."

Jake took her in his arms again, lingering in the warmth of the sun against their bodies. He took one last taste of her with him before she thrust her voice recorder into his hands. "Make sure you let Carter know I have that backed up on my computer, and it won't do any good for him to destroy it."

"That is the last thing we want him to know, unless we are going to spend all our nights like last night."

"Yeah, I can see how you wouldn't want to agree to that."

"You can't see anything, and I'm still not telling him there's another copy."

Jake kissed her again, then climbed into the cab of the truck.

Spitting gravel down the road behind him, Jake drove for the alfalfa field. The closer he drew to the chore the more his instincts felt heavy. *Will Carter take her, too?* He wondered as her form disappeared in the rearview mirror.

Jake parked the truck near the wire gate that closed off the field. No one would come and steal alfalfa, but the watering system was another thing all together. He moved quickly, unhooking the pvc pipes from the larger pipe.

Rolling the wagon wheels that transported the system, Jake reset the spigots and moved back to the gate to hook up the pipes. Once the water was flowing and Jake could see that the placement was right, he relocked the gate and climbed back into the truck. None of his calls were any more fruitful than they had been this morning, and Jake tossed the phone into the glove box and put the recorder in his jeans pocket.

One of the sprayers was stuck pointing north, and Jake watched it for a moment to see if it would resume its pattern. When it didn't, Jake shook his thoughts loose from Cassie and Carter and made his way through the alfalfa to the sprinkler.

The morning light was blinding off the steel sprinklers, which might have been why Jake had not seen the truck pull up beside his. The persistent and monotonous sound of the sprinkling system disguised its approach as well, so Jake was unaware of the truck's occupants before he came face to face with them.

"Jake," Carter growled in his face. "Imagine my surprise when my Uncle Ed called and told me you accused me of pranking your little blind friend. Imagine how upset that makes me. It is a good thing I showed up at The Rocking J early enough this morning to see you kissing her good-bye."

"Cassie has nothing to do with this. You could have gotten her killed last night over that recording. Stay away from her, Carter. She is no threat to you."

"Oh, I know that Jake. She's just entertainment. We had bad timing this morning, that's all. She won't be any fun, and me and Diego showed up too early to late with you. Luckily for Cassie, I also saw her give the recorder to you so there was no reason to bother her for it."

"Carter, I'm not interested in involving anyone else in this mess." Jake glanced over Carter's shoulder at the large Mexican ranch hand glowering from the road. "Let's just work this out, the two of us. Forget about Cassie and Diego, and tell me what you want." Carter cocked back his fist, and Jake ducked away from the unprovoked attack. "I told you before; fighting with me will only make your chances with the women worse."

With no warning, Carter launched himself toward where Jake stood, and the two of them rolled in a jumble of feet and fists toward the tree lined edge of the road. They came to their feet at the same time, but Carter overbalanced and Jake managed to throw him off before crouching on the balls of his feet, his fists balled in front of his face. Carter slid in the gravel, then rose slowly spitting dirt and blood from a split lip, fury burning in his eyes. "This can't be settled between us, Jake. Your Cassie recorded me talking about that fire."

As Carter danced closer, Jake saw Diego moving toward him from the side. He couldn't see clearly, but the big man looked as if he held a baseball bat wrapped in barbed wire in one hand. Jake took the recorder out of his pocket and offered it to Carter, keeping a fair distance from both approaching men. "Here's your confession, Carter. No one has heard it, and there're no copies. Take it, leave Cassie alone, and you and I can finish this like men."

Carter slapped the handheld recorder from where Jake held it out to him, and crushed it beneath the heel of his boot. "Finish this? It will never be finished until one of us is dead. It was my turn that night on the mountain, but you had to play the hero. Now it's your turn and Casanova can't save you."

Carter spit blood into the gravel again, plunging forward to grab Jake's torso. Twisting to avoid the direct hit, Jake saw in his peripheral the flash of metal from beside him. He took the body blow Carter gave him, collapsing to the ground beneath the man's weight to avoid the swing of the bat in Diego's hand.

Jake hit the road on his back, using his legs to pitch Carter over his head toward Diego. The momentum of Carter's body carried them both toward the river. Jake rolled over backward and came to his feet again, facing both Carter and Diego.

The two fuming assailants crowded in on Jake as he wiped blood from off his eyebrow. Jake's senses were taut; his muscles strained in expectancy, but not for the last sight that met his eyes.

Silver light glinted and a blur of movement erupted across Jake's mind as the thick wooden bat strung with wire and bent nails ripped the air between them. Jake reflexively turned his face to the side and braced himself for impact. Jake didn't feel the tearing flesh or spurting blood; he felt only the caress of willow branches on his cheek as he fell, and darkness engulfed him.

*

A whisper drifted through the willow branches and roused his heavy eyelids to flutter. Jake forced open his eyes and tried to clear his mind. It could not have been the trees swishing above him and the lilted lullaby of the creek beside him that stirred questions in his head. Harsher sounds finally breaking through his foggy thoughts confirmed his suspicion that he had heard something else. A smatter of sprinklers hissing in the distance, sparked more awareness, but he sought for what had tugged on his mind.

Still reaching for the absent sound, Jake's instincts sharpened and he immediately became aware that he was supposed to be moving the watering system on the alfalfa field every hour. His mind was bogged down in a muddy cloud of swirling confusion as he tried to focus. His thoughts would not collect but seemed to run in all directions as if being flung by the powerful sprinklers, too far away to grasp.

In the distorted darkness, Jake's mind did allow him the brief image of his father's dark, disapproving scowl. Even in his sleepy haze, Jake could feel the man's glare at his carelessness with the new alfalfa.

As he attempted to rise from the moist creek bank to attend the field, he was instantly doused in a blinding flash of white hot pain behind his eyes. With a groan, that seemed to reverberate in his brain like thunder to his pounding skull, Jake rolled onto his stomach, pressing his hands into the damp earth, before pushing up to his hands and knees. A wave of nausea stole breath from his lungs as the creek and bank tilted and the overhanging branches of the willow seemed to be reaching down to force him back against the dirt.

Jake sank onto his chest and moaned again as he lay his throbbing head onto the shore of the bubbling stream. His vision swam in a whirlpool of colors until he focused on the crimson stain beneath his throbbing jaw. Pooling in a puddle beside his cheek, blood ran deep into the broken soil, and Jake flinched as its meaning caught hold in his heart. The soft sound of that crying wind met his pulsating ears once more, and Jake closed his eyes against awareness.

"Jake!" the wind screamed this time. "Jake, if you can hear me, make some noise." The voice was frantic, broken syllables caught between high pressure sprays of water and the unbearable pain in his head. *It was too far away,* he thought with another silent moan, as the sound was chased by the brisk wind above the branches of the trees.

The hot August wind brushed across his dry lips as Jake rolled onto his back, knowing somewhere in his pounding brain he needed to call out to the drifting voice. The parched condition of his throat did not elicit sound, and the attempt screamed glassy shards of pain throughout his aching skull.

Something sticky pressed against his jaw, and Jake tried to move his mouth to shake it loose, only to discover the white hot pain tearing consciousness away from the closing presence of that voice. The slight but jerky movements he had been able to accomplish now stole thought, energy, and voice from his desperate need to make some sound so someone would find him. The darkness began to close around him, as if he was being dragged backward through a tunnel, swallowing him.

Chapter Eighteen

"Jake?" Cassie whispered his name into the hot afternoon. There was no breeze, but maybe its sound could still find him. She finished rubbing Jackpot down and gave the mare a handful of kale, Miriam had given her after lunch. Listening to the horses contented chomping, Cassie could almost pretend that the world still felt the same to her. Her mind couldn't even form that thought without her heart protesting. There was so much of this with Jake that raised the hackles of her protective instincts. Her mind warned her heart to be wary of him; she was falling faster and more thoroughly than she thought possible.

She and Dylan had worked together for nearly a year before he took notice of her. He was careful, quiet, and thoughtful. His strength and confidence attracted her more than anything else. In retrospect, the long pauses in conversation seemed more deceptive than patient. The hesitation she felt from him was more tactical than tender. The feeling had been different from this one, but never having fallen in love before, Cassie didn't know that there was a difference. She had been drawn to Dylan's strength, believing it was who he was. With Jake it was his vulnerability, and the immense power he possessed in spite of it. She believed he truly was a good man, not just the appearance of one.

Jackpot nuzzled against Cassie with a velvet nose and Cassie buried her face in the dusty smell of the horse's mane. *Where are you, Jake?* she thought.

"Hey, Cassie," Troy's voice brought her out of her reverie. "Sheriff Harris is on the phone up at the house for you. Do you want me to take you up there or should I just have Jana take a message?"

"He's just following up with me on the rattlesnake. Tell him I haven't remembered anything new, and I haven't seen or heard any more trouble."

She listened to Troy swearing under his breath and then his footsteps as he walked away. This morning after Jake left, Cassie had filled Troy and Miriam in on the night before, and Troy was fairly irate about the sheriff's handling of the situation. This would give Troy the opportunity to let Ed Harris hear exactly what he wanted to say.

Turning her back on the rail fence, Cassie leaned back and held her hair off the nape of her neck. It would probably top 110 degrees today. Maybe when Jake came back, they could go to the reservoir. Her afternoon with the MS kids had been postponed until Monday so her time was free. She could use some one-on-one time with both Jake and Jackpot; the reservoir would provide enough privacy and space for both.

Panicked footsteps couldn't be disguised. They hurry and hesitate all at once. Troy's footsteps were still measured as he approached Cassie's perch on the fence, but her heart immediately heard the alarm in them.

"The sheriff wasn't checking on you," Troy panted. "He said to warn you or Jake that he questioned Carter this morning, and when Carter left the office he was looking for a fight."

"When was that?"

"He said a couple of hours ago."

"A couple of hours! That's enough time for him to have killed Jake by now. The sheriff thought a phone call *a few hours later* was appropriate?"

Cassie pushed the button on her talking watch and gasped at the announcement of 12:45.

"Troy, get the truck and your two-way radios. Jake's up at Caswell Farms northwestern alfalfa field. If Carter is looking for him, we may have enough time to find him first. If we have to split up, I need to be able to talk to you, though."

Cassie grabbed her cane from the fence beside her and began following Troy's boots on the gravel.

"How far away is the field?" Cassie asked, urgently.

"It's probably only a few miles, but the access road is rough, and it might take a while to get there."

"Do you have four-wheel drive?"

"Yes, ma'am."

"That's all we need; we have to get to that field."

*

Cassie climbed into Troy's truck and pulled out her cell phone. First she called Jana at the ranch house and told her where they were going. She called the sheriff's office to keep emergency services on alert, but was informed that EMS was only on alert if you reported an emergency. Cassie didn't have anything concrete to report. For all she knew, Jake was fighting with stubborn waterlines and she was panicking over nothing. The sinking pit in her stomach argued the rational thoughts, and Cassie held firmly to the radio Troy had given her for confidence.

A half hour later Troy's four-wheel drive kicked in, and Cassie lost all orientation to direction as they bumped along the access road north of the field.

"I see one of Caswell's trucks by the gate, but I don't see Jake or anyone else."

"How high is the alfalfa this time of year? Could he be in the field?"

"He could be, but the water is on, so he'd be awfully wet."

The truck slid to a stop, and Cassie jumped from the cab.

"Jake! Are you here?"

"It looks like someone was here. There are fresh tire tracks, it looks like another truck."

"Jake! If you can hear me make some noise so I can find you."

Cassie heard Troy's footsteps moving down the road further, and she turned her face into the slight wind that wound from the willows. She could smell the water, alfalfa, and a salty wetness. Cassie wrinkled her brow and tried to sort out the sounds and smells pulsating around her. The pit in her stomach was disconcerting her as she focused on the hint of a sound. Taking one hesitant step toward the gurgle of a nearby river, Cassie heard the moan of an injured animal just beyond her. The salty smell turned rusty and tasted of blood.

"Jake!" she screamed, hearing the sound more distinctly.

Cassie scrambled toward the noise, collapsing to her hands and knees when the tangle of willows slapped against her face. Her thoughts scrambled nearly as desperately as she did as she found the edge of a riverbank and slid down onto the damp ground beneath the tree. Movement and a pain-filled groan led her hands to the thick curling of what she immediately recognized as Jake's hair. He moaned, and tried to move toward her but she put her hands against his chest.

"Shhh, baby, hold still, you're hurt, and I don't know what's wrong yet."

Cassie cautiously touched his forehead and scalp, finding only a surface cut above his eyebrow. She felt across his cheeks and down his jaw, until her fingers brushed the ragged edge of damp skin and mud. She moved beyond the wound to his neck, throat, and then his chest but found no other wounds. His chest was unmarred and his arms and legs seemed to be as strong as ever. Jake kept trying to push himself up from the riverbank only to collapse with the effort.

"Lie still, Jake, you'll make it worse. Your jaw might be broken, and there's blood everywhere. Hold on, and I'll get help."

Cassie pulled the two-way radio from her pocket and reported her location to Troy. Troy promised he would get the ambulance and sheriff before disconnecting.

"I told you I would track you down." Cassie told him as she held onto his hand. "Technically I'm an hour or so early, but I couldn't wait any longer. Ever since we killed Casanova last night, I haven't been able to keep away from you."

Cassie felt her heart tearing with the sounds Jake was making in response, and she put her hand over his lips. "Don't talk. The way I see it you are stuck listening to me say I told you so, and you are helpless to fight back."

Luckily, in Lindley the ambulance was a pick-up truck so the rough road held no insurmountable obstacles in getting to them. Once Jake had been strapped to a backboard and hooked to an IV, Cassie let go of his hand and let them load him in the truck. She and Troy followed them back to the emergency clinic, where they waited beside a paper curtain for news.

*

Robert and Debra Caswell showed up, and Cassie and Troy did their best to explain what they knew, which wasn't much. Debra wanted to know if Jake had been unconscious beside the river all night long, since he had never gotten around to making a phone call to his mom. Robert timidly informed Debra that Jake had checked in with him about the alfalfa field and the truck, and he forgot to report it to Debra. Cassie was grateful for Robert's confession; it kept her from having to explain to Debra why Jake had not come home last night.

In a small town like Lindley, the news of their golden boy being attacked spread like wild fire. The waiting area was full of Casanova's admirers, as well as Jake's friends and family. Despite her ignorance of how many people were listening or who they were, Cassie did not want to talk about her and Jake with any of them.

Hours passed interminably and most of the spectators moved on. Troy filed a report with Sheriff Harris, then returned to The Rocking J.

In the quiet that followed, Cassie told Robert and Debra everything they knew about the fire, Carter, the rattler, and Jake's plans to talk to Carter.

"Why didn't he tell me about any of that when he talked to me about the field this morning?" Robert fumed. "The only reason I've been helping that Langdon kid is because I know Jake feels responsible to that family. It's good for the boy to accept responsibility, but if I had known Carter was this big of a problem, I would have kept him as far from Jake as I could."

"Jake never wanted it to be that big of a deal. I think he believed Carter would eventually figure out the truth and leave him alone," Cassie said.

"He thought that deeply about it?" Debra asked, quirking an eyebrow.

"Jake does a lot more thinking than people know," Cassie said. She felt the eyes of Jake's parents on her, and the heat bloomed in her cheeks.

Cassie heard the squeak of wheels, and Debra jumped to her feet as a nurse pushed a rolling bed past Cassie. As they passed her, Cassie felt Jake take her hand so tightly that she was forced to follow him.

She figured Robert and Debra were somewhere nearby, but she heard and felt only the pound of her own pulse and the digital beep of Jake's heart monitor in her ears.

"Well, it's not as bad as it looked," a voice was explaining. "The weapon cut through some tissue and muscle along his jaw line, but severed no major arteries and didn't break his jaw. He is going to be sore for a long while. He'll need to be on a liquid diet for about a week and avoid too much talking, but he should recover with nothing but a wicked scar for memories. The CAT scan showed no swelling or bleeding on his brain, but he'll have one heck of a headache that should be treated with ibuprofen every four hours. He will need the dressing on the stitches replaced every day, and we will remove them in a week to ten days. Any questions?"

Robert and Debra began barraging the doctor with follow-up questions, but Cassie just held onto Jake's hand. When the doctor had mentioned "the wicked scar," Jake's grip faltered and slipped out of Cassie's grasp. She was holding it again, but it was weak and flaccid beneath her fingers, and Cassie wondered if the pain medicine had taken effect. He was still and silent in the bed, and Cassie thought about slipping away.

As she moved away from his side, Ed Harris joined them. Cassie smelled the distinct aroma of his Stetson cologne before she heard his voice and stiffened automatically.

"If Jake can't talk for a while," Ed drawled. "We can wait to take his statement. He's got a pretty bad head injury, though, and his recollections might not be reliable."

"Jake's head is fine," Robert snapped. "He can write down all you need without talking."

"Of course, Robert. I just thought he might want to clear his mind for a few days before he files the report, that's all."

Cassie heard the sleeping volcano in Robert Caswell's heart begin to percolate, and she jumped in before they were all caught in the eruption.

"Sheriff Harris, from what I heard in the waiting room today, you will be getting a number of complaints from local women about Carter's behavior. Whatever Jake has to say about this is just one of Carter's worries. He will be facing sexual assault charges along with attempted murder and arson, too."

"Now, Miss Taylor, we do things around here a little differently than in the city. Folks don't jump the law on every good ol' boy who gets a little drunk and stupid."

"Caswell Farm is part of a federal land grant, Sheriff. That makes the stable fire a case of federal property destruction at the least. This is out of your hands now, and I have a copy of Carter admitting to the fire in a digital file on my computer. If you're prepared to have federal scrutiny on your police department procedures, then be my guest. Do your investigation like one of the good ol' boys, but understand that Carter nearly killed him twice and it stops now."

Cassie bent over and kissed the top of Jake's head, ignoring the jerk of him flinching. Picking up her cane, she swung it broadly and listened as the room's occupants cleared out of her way.

Chapter Nineteen

"Jake," Cassie snapped. "Hold still so I don't hurt you."

Jake caught her hands in his and glared into her unseeing expression.

"I can change the bandages myself, Cass. Leave it alone."

"I know you can, Jake. I just wanted to feel how it's doing. I'll be careful, I promise."

"Leave it, Cassie. I get the stitches out tomorrow. I don't need the reminder that it's there."

Cassie made a face at him, then moved to the other side of the porch swing. Jake had been home for a while, but between the swelling and the stitches, communication between them had been difficult at best. Now, with the cut healing and his jaw stiff but moveable, he didn't have silence to hide behind anymore.

"What's wrong, Jake, are you in pain?"

"Nothing is wrong. I have the same decisions to make as I did before. Carter tried to knock my head off, and I have new problems to consider."

"What kind of new problems?"

"My deadline for the land grant was extended, but I'm committed in September so it won't do me any good. My face is not exactly the poster boy that modeling agencies are looking for; and I can't even look in the mirror anymore without triggering nightmares. Is that enough or do you need more?"

Jake watched Cassie's expression harden under his flinging of hurtful words, and he flinched away from it. She had been with him through the whole mess. Women had come out of the woodwork to file charges against Carter, and Lilly had even showed up to make a report. There was an official investigation into Carter's activities on the farm, and Carter was in hiding until it ended up resolved or charges were prosecuted. Either way, it was because of her turning her sim card over to the arson investigator and filing reports with the sheriff that Carter was finished harassing both of them.

She hadn't left his side during his recovery. She'd made him milkshakes and mashed potatoes. She was tender, patient, and constant. But he couldn't explain to her what was really bothering him. She saw him the same, her mental picture of him had not changed. How could he explain how traumatic it was for him to look in the mirror and see only the line of marred flesh along his jaw? There would never be the rough and rugged look for him again. The crooked line would part his unshaven features leaving a permanent scar. How could he explain it to her?

"Cassie, I'm sorry. I'm not ready to talk about this. Can we leave it alone?"

"What were we talking about that you're not ready for Jake? I asked if you were in pain."

Jake gritted his teeth and his jaw screamed at him for his thoughtlessness. He must have made a sound because Cassie quickly moved toward him and then caught herself.

"If you aren't in pain, you have a funny way of showing it."

"This isn't going to work, Cassie. You can't possibly understand what I'm dealing with, and I can't explain. Things changed. I changed. You can't help me. You can't even see what is bothering me."

"What can't I see, Jake?"

"My horribly scarred and disfigured face; you'll tell me how it doesn't matter, and you never saw my face anyway, but that's the problem. How could you understand when none of it matters to you? It matters to me because I have to look in the mirror and see the expressions of everyone who sees the scar. It makes a difference to me. Maybe that makes me less of a man, but it matters."

"Just because I don't see faces doesn't mean I don't understand that they are important."

"I can't do this with you, Cassie, it's like complaining to a cancer patient that I have a paper cut. I need to figure me out, alone."

Cassie got off the swing and took her cane from where it leaned against the wall of The Rocking J's ranch house. Placing it against the wall where the porch met the house, she walked away from him toward the front door.

"I understand plenty. I'm blind, not stupid. I'll see ya around, Casanova."

Jake fought back a wave of sharpened truth, slicing its way into his heart. She had never called him that, and the sting of its ragged truth cut him deeply. He watched her go around the corner and listened as her footsteps climbed the stairs to her apartment. The dark feelings were eating at him, something beyond that she was literally blind to his problems. He knew she would make him look at it differently; she'd been doing that since the day he met her. The truth of that terrified him. If she made him look at it differently, then she would be seeing something different too. Even the thought of her touching his face sent chills down his spine, and he had come tonight to send her away.

He prepared himself for anger, tears, disappointment. Most women he knew met his breakups with those reactions. She had called him Casanova. Somehow the use of his nickname left him cold in the hot August heat. She already saw him differently.

Jake drove the Mitsubishi home that night under the watchful gaze of Cassiopeia once more. That night all those months ago, she had seemed so volatile and unsteady. Now as he gazed up at the pale blue light that hovered around her stars, Jake saw the constancy of Cassie's sight.

*

With the stitches removed and the sun evening out the tan on his skin, the scar loomed like a pale light across his face. He thought it would get better, but everywhere he went he saw people's eyes inadvertently drawn to it. His eyes were constantly drawn to it, too: in the bathroom fixtures, when he glanced in the rearview mirror, he couldn't escape it; the scar itself even haunted his dreams.

Cassie called him the day after he got his stitches out, just to check on him, she said. He had seen her occasionally when he picked up Heidi, but she never sought him out, and he never gave her the chance. His chest ached every time he saw her, the sadness in her eyes affirming his worst fears. He was classified with Dylan now. He could understand why Dylan had been too much of a coward to face her. Those haunting blue eyes had the ability to make him feel naked in front of her.

Staring into his own indigo gaze in the bar back at Mcgoo's, Jake pictured the gazing eyes to be hers instead, knowing too much. His phone vibrated in his pocket and Jake took his concentration off the reflection to answer.

"Jake, it's Gary. I heard about your troubles out there. Are you okay?"

"I'm fine, Gary, but things have changed, and we need to get together and talk."

"Changed? Jake, don't change anything. I have you booked in New Zealand in a week and a half. The director saw that scar of yours and can't wait to get you in this movie."

"He wants me scarred?"

"Not scarred, man, ruggedly sexy. A man with a scar is only more desirable. Yours actually would have been better if it were more obvious. That little line on your jaw is barely noticeable, and the director wants to see if he can extend it across your cheek or something. So don't tell me you changed your mind."

The music and noise of the bar began to pound in Jake's head, drowning out Gary's prattle, and Jake closed his phone and glanced back up at his reflection.

Natalie Harper's green eyes lit the mirrored view behind him. He refused to smile. This was one thing that hadn't changed. He figured with the new face staring back at her, Natalie would be the first one of his "friends" to run from the horror.

Yet, here she was, that hungry look in her green eyes and the want surging off her body.

"Jake. I'm so happy to see you back here. Let me look at you."

Natalie spun the stool until he faced her, stepping between his knees, and running her long manicured fingers through his hair.

"You don't look much the worse for wear," she quipped sweetly. "Still as gorgeous as always, maybe a little more tired, but hot as ever."

Jake cocked a half smile at her, not able to ignore the compliment. "Thanks, Nat. It's good to be seen."

"I'll bet. It must have been pure torture for a man like you to have spent the last few months with someone who could never see what she had."

"What are you babbling about?" Jake grumbled pushing her away from him. He felt the guilty flush of his cheeks with Natalie's reference to Cassie.

"You wasted all these months on that blind woman when you should have been here, with me. I know exactly what a catch you are. I have to admit, I was a little worried at first. You chasing after her, but I get it now."

Jake leaned his elbows on the bar and scrutinized her perfect features. "Get what?"

"Casanova. You hook yourself up with a blind woman, and everyone thinks you are the responsible, charismatic, loving, good boy. You come here and flirt, dance, make out, or whatever, and you live both lives. She is totally oblivious and what she can't see won't hurt her, while the rest of us have nice, steamy weekends and one-night stands to look forward to."

Jake swallowed hard and narrowed his eyes to see if she was kidding. Was this some new plan of attack? The blatant desperation wasn't working so she was going for casual mistress?

"Are you telling me you don't care who else I'm with, you just want to be on the list?"

"Casanova's list is the main desire of every girl in here, Jake. I am one of the few that understand. You either take a spot on it, or you stay off."

Natalie tossed her hair back from her eyes and moved toward him again, placing her hand on his thigh.

"I want to take the top spot Jake, but I don't want to be limited to just one any more than you do. This can work for both of us."

Jake smiled, and the light that filled Natalie's eyes showed him she thought she had him, hook, line, and sinker. "It all makes sense now, Natalie; why only I can see the scar. It is not the ugliest part of me. It's not the scar I hate looking at; that scar is all I can see, because I can't stand looking at Casanova."

Jake stood up from his stool so quickly, Natalie stumbled backward in surprise. Jake wrapped both arms around her to keep her from falling, then hugged her against him.

"You're right, about all of it. You brilliant, beautiful girl."

Natalie giggled against him momentarily as Jake pushed her back again. "Oh, Natalie I wish I could warn the others."

"Warn the others about what?"

Jake twirled one of her long blond curls around his finger, trailed the tip of it down her neck, and then stared, deep into her emerald eyes. "That you are nothing but candy-covered misery."

"What does that mean? Where are you going?"

"To have a girl look at my face," Jake shouted as he rushed for the swinging doors of the bar.

Chapter Twenty

"Jake," Cassie snapped acidly. "His name is Jake. Not 'that guy,' 'the actor,' or 'Casanova.'"

Cassie had not formed a picture in her mind of what the new counselor looked like, but in the dark recesses of her heart, Cassie imagined the unknown girl's lip quivering with the rebuke. Cassie wasn't waiting around for weary smiles and comments to part the thick awkwardness dampening the air on the front porch of The Rocking J. She grabbed her cane from its position against the porch rail, banging her way down the stairs and around the corner of the ranch house.

When Miriam asked her to show the new girl, Shelly, around this afternoon, Cassie had reluctantly agreed. *What good is a tour by a blind person?* Cassie wondered. *Someone who can show her everything should be doing this.*

Cassie turned back, prepared to stalk to her steps, the red fury of Shelly's question still boiling her blood.

"Does that actor guy, Casanova, hang out here much?" Cassie mocked in a high-pitched whine. "Can I fall all over him and make a fool of myself?"

The sound of Jana's voice explaining Cassie's outburst to Shelly brought on a flood of tears, and Cassie paused, unable to force herself back to the house.

The night was hot, and her eyes felt dry and heavy despite the crying. Fleeing from the distant voices, unable to escape her own thoughts, Cassie counted her steps to the fence, then followed it into the aspens. The small dirt path leading to the creek below the fields was crisply clear in her mind, and under her cane as she found the gurgling sounds of the nearby water.

Cassie figured it was close to full night by now. The tour hadn't taken long, and she was secretly grateful that Miriam had forced her out tonight. Cassie would never let her work suffer. She went on as usual with the horses and her clients, but she was different since her conversation with Jake. What had given her away? She held her emotions from her attitude and stayed behind her apartment door, thinking it the best way to keep from burdening the rest with her regret and tears. It evidently hadn't worked though. Miriam knew, and no one seemed surprised tonight when she snapped at Shelly's innocent question about everyone's favorite local superstar.

A part of her intellectual mind told her that this was good. She must be dealing with her betrayal if she couldn't hide it. Technically, she was rebounding from Dylan. This brutal reminder of what was wrong with men would prepare her to make better decisions in the future.

The problem was this didn't feel like a rebound. She had no leftover emotions from Dylan. This hadn't resurrected hate, anger, or even love for her past. This was all Jake.

Cassie stumbled onto the rocky edge of the small creek, before wiping at her wet cheeks. A warm wind blew through the creek bed, and Cassie sank down beside the sound of bubbling water to immerse herself in the sounds, smells and feelings from the night. If she couldn't take her mind off him, she would lose herself in feelings that harbored peaceful images in her thoughts. She began tossing pebbled rocks at her feet into the water, listening to the pleasant sound of plopping as they sank beneath the surface.

The texture of the moist ground beneath her palms drew her fingers into the earth; she balled her hands into fists to gather the grimy sand in them. The feeling of gritty roughness felt like a thousand pinpricks in her hands, and Cassie focused on the minute sensations. She needed to feel something besides the ache in her heart. She hadn't had him that long, why the big deal? None of it had been real, anyway. She was being foolish to feel this way. She knew all along whom she was dealing with.

The arguments felt like the sizzle of oil on her burning mind. It didn't matter how long it had taken, or how short it lasted, she had let go and . . . fallen for him?

A fresh onslaught of tears ran down her cheeks as she plunged her hands into the cool water, rinsing the sand from beneath her nails. She had fallen for him; for his humor, his intensity, his goodness. She had fallen in love with him. Despite her best efforts to avoid it, she had. *Casanova,* her mind tortured.

"Jake," she whispered. "His name is Jake."

"Promise me I'm the Jake you're talking about."

Cassie jumped to her feet, heart pounding, and feet scrambling for the river bank. Hands, his hands, grabbed her arms and held her firmly, until she found her footing.

"That's not the name you called me the last time we talked."

"The last thing you heard me call you is preferable to what I have called you since then."

His deep throaty laugh was mirthless, and she shook his hold on her away.

"I probably deserved every one of them. I just hope the fact that you are calling my name again is a good thing."

"Stick around," she retorted. "You can hear me call you much worse."

Jake cleared his throat and stepped away from her, as she crossed her arms over her chest. "I probably deserve that, too, so I think I'll stay."

"Fine, Jake. Have it your way."

Cassie turned her back on him and slid back onto the bank of the creek. "I didn't hear anyone on the trail, I thought I was alone."

"Only if you want to be. Miriam told me where to find you. I need a favor."

"What kind of favor, Jake?" Cassie asked, wiping her still damp hands across her cheeks and slipping further down on the creek's edge. She listened as he came to sit beside her, reeling with his sudden presence. She couldn't handle him here, asking her to set him up with the new girl, or telling her he was leaving.

Cassie sunk her hands back into the river mud to keep them from shaking. *Why is he here? What does he want?*

"Monday I need to make a trip to Carson City, but Heidi has an appointment with you and Applesauce that morning. Could I reschedule?"

"Talk to Miriam or Troy. We can make arrangements for Heidi to go back to the farm without you here."

"Oh, Heidi's coming with me."

"That's fine, Jake. She is doing really well; we can either reschedule or skip Monday. It doesn't matter."

Jake cleared his throat uncomfortably and she felt his fingers moving through the dirt where she buried hers. Before she could pull away from him, Jake was holding her hand in his, the mud pressing grittily between their entwined fingers.

"I was hoping you might be able to clear your schedule that day, too. I'd like you to come along."

"Why?" Cassie snapped, yanking her hand free. "What's so important in Carson City?"

"I'm filing the paperwork for the land grant on Monday. It's not that big of a deal, mostly. I just can't stand being away from you any longer."

Cassie moved down the creek bank as far as she dared go. "What's your game now, Jake? Heidi won't go with you unless I go, too? You can't get your land unless I fix this for you?"

"Cassie, I messed everything up. I know that, and fixing is going to take time and trust, but I swear to you this is not a game."

"Words, Jake. Empty words and more of your Casanova crap. I'm not interested."

He moved so swiftly. He was beside her, his hands holding her, his breath warm on her skin.

"There's no Casanova left, that's what I'm trying to tell you. I held onto a part of that because I wasn't sure what I wanted. When Carter scarred my face, I thought the decision would be made for me. You didn't care, my face looks the same to you no matter what, but then I realized it wouldn't. With that scar in place, you would be able to see Casanova, too."

Cassie shook her head to fight back the tears she felt running down her cheeks. "I don't, Jake, I never have. You have always been Jake to me."

"I know," he said softly brushing at her tears with his muddy fingers. "You will be able to feel the ugly on my face now though. That piece of me that didn't die when I fell in love with you got out and took up permanent residence on my jaw. Every time you run your fingers through my hair, you will see that night you first saw me." He wound his fingers through her tangled locks, and she shuddered with his touch. "Every time you touch my lips or kiss me, you'll see the real me, but every time you touch that scar you will see Casanova. The thought of you seeing me like that, I couldn't take that chance. You taught me that life, dreams, and love are a chance, and I want to take it with you."

Cassie was shaking her head. Jake wound his fingers in her hair more securely. Brushing her cheeks with his thumbs, he held her face between his palms.

"Look at me Cassie, please."

"I can't Jake. I can't touch you again, it hurts too much."

Cassie felt his mouth on her cheeks, his lips kissing sweetly through her tears. "I love you Cassie. Try to see the truth."

Cassie braced her arms against the moist earth, closing her eyes and fighting the emotions that she had convinced herself she wouldn't give him.

"Jake, please don't do this to me again. The only fight I have left is to forget. If I look at you, I will never forget. Your face will always haunt me. Isn't it enough that I fell for Casanova? Do you need this?"

"Everyone falls for Casanova; he's shallow and easy. I want you to see if you can want the real me."

As her fingers ran swiftly over his face, dirt, grit, and tiny pebbles kept her from feeling skin beneath her palms. Compelling her senses deeper, she groped for the form and shape of his features. Without intending to, Cassie released her fear into a world of light and form. Before she knew it was happening, she painted a picture in her mind; deep azure eyes, looking longingly into hers. High cheekbones, a perfect smile framed by tender lips, the strong mouth and jaw of the man from her dreams.

"Jake," she choked. "I can see you."

"I know, baby. Can you live with this ugly mug?"

"I love you, Jake. I can't live without it."

"I'm never leaving, Cass. I'm staying on Mustang Mountain. I know who I am. I've been discovered by a blind woman."

"Not discovered," she teased against his mouth. "Just uncovered."

The sounds and smells of the creek side faded into the night as Jake took her in his arms and kissed her. It was not the same as the first time; she never even thought about slowing down now. Her mind filled with flashes of white hot light and sweet satin flavors, and she knew she could finally see what true love looked like.

About the Author

Traci McDonald lives in scenic southern Utah with her husband and three sons. Besides her writing, she loves family history, books in any form, and music.

Despite having lost her eyesight 17 years ago, Traci plays softball with her husband, rides a tandem bicycle, and enjoys movies (as long as she can ask questions along the way).

You can e-mail her at tracimcdonaldauthor@gmail.com, read her blog at tracimcdonald.blogspot.com, or on Facebook at Traci McDonald, Ivins, Utah.

In the mood for more Crimson Romance? Check out *Caution: Filling Is Hot* by Tara Mills at *CrimsonRomance.com*.